A VERY FAIRY CHRISTMAS

First Edition. December 15, 2023
Copyright © 2023 Tiana Renatus
Written by Tiana Renatus
Cover design by GetCovers (a part of the Miblgroup family of brands).

A Very Fairy Christmas

(a Tropes Are Us universe story)
By: Tiana Renatus
First Edition, 2023

Prologue

"Red and gold must be bound before the Cold Moon. The story started with love, and it must end with it. Even magic needs a second chance sometimes to make the right choice."

Farren Jeffries paused to look at the old witch who suddenly appeared at the edge of the garden. "Leina, I didn't realize you were there. Nina is very grateful—"

"Pain will buzz, and fear will smother before the truth can be seen glistening on a sharp blade."

Nodding slowly, he refrained from speaking in case she had more to share. All in Karsia knew of magic and interrupting a witch was the quickest way to feel that power. The grey-haired elder offered him a bag while staring at him with eyes Farren was sure changed colors. "Thank you."

"You will not wish to thank me when you walk in your own footsteps. But it is the second bloom that is the sweetest. You must remember that."

She disappeared before his eyes and his ears popped. Farren blinked and shook his head. "Son of a banshee, magic is getting out of hand here."

"Farren, Farren!"

The child calling to him soon collided with Farren's legs. He scooped her up despite her excited squirming.

"There is a fairy in Karsia. I saw his wings. We have a fairy!"

"I think we 'have' a fairy, Lady Lilly. There is a lot of unexplained magic and we—"

"You must go see him. He is asking for you." The child managed to land on her feet only to jump up and down again. "Mama said to get you fast as a pixie!"

He followed the child back into town but dropped her off at her house before moving closer to the crowd who hid the stranger from Farren's gaze. However, he heard the words over the din.

"I have coins but only need one to give me information."

Farren smirked when no one accepted the deal – fairies were notorious tricksters after all. The newcomer left standing alone stole Farren's breath with his beauty. His uniform fitted his body to reveal power and grace with each step. While he'd never heard of fairies being warriors, this one was tall, strong, and had an impressive sword strapped to his hips. His glittery wings cast a surprisingly large shadow against his back. He waited until it was close enough to hear him. "Food would have been a better bribe as no one is dumb enough to take a fairy deal."

The fairy stopped in front of him with a quiet huff. "It was not a bribe, nor am I making deals. I do not need the gratitude of your kind. I only need information."

"So, ask me." Farren wasn't sure why he offered. Magic was part of his world, but it always brought problems and dangers. There was no guarantee this being was a fairy. It was obvious he was magical and powerful...and gorgeous. "Maybe I'll take the coins."

Silver eyes met his and, for just a second, Farren could almost see a sparkling glow of magic surrounding the fairy. Instead of the translucent silver of his wings, a brilliant array of colors flashed quickly and then disappeared.

"I'm looking for a guide. The name I have is Farren Jeffries."

Hearing his name in the deep, musical voice sent a stab of desire through his body. "Today is your lucky day, Princeling. Now, put those wings away and we'll discuss business."

Chapter 1

"Why am I in a human hospital?" Cabel Orlaith frowned when the nurse partially shifted to her Wolverine form. "That is not an appropriate answer, beast. Run along and find someone with more authority and knowledge."

She stomped away leaving him alone in the drab room. There was nothing visible to spark any recognition of the facility. His last memory...a hazy blank space sent his heart racing. His magic only fluttered weakly which meant another shot of adrenaline left his skin tingling. It was then he noticed the man standing in the doorway. Nothing about the man said medical professional – his brown pants were too tight, muddy boots covered the lower half of his legs, and the tee shirt under the open button-down appeared stained. Cabel's heart calmed during his perusal, and he took a deep breath. The scent of pine and snow filled his nostrils with nostalgic warmth. *Agoen* was almost always snow-covered, and he missed his homeland every time he visited the human realm. A fuzzy thought disappeared too quickly for him to process it, but it left Cabel with an even deeper yearning for home. He glared at the human still loitering in his line of sight. "I do not believe you are a healer. State your business or leave."

Straightening from his slumped position, the scruffy man stared at him without speaking.

"Do I know you?" Cabel again found his mind teasing him with something important, something just out of reach.

"No, it appears you don't. Take care of yourself, Princling."

"Princeling?" Cabel tried to push up to stand, but his body screamed in agony. He flopped back in an undignified heap. Lifting a hand to his pounding heart and struggling lungs, the presence of a scratchy, human fabric distracted him. It was green, ill-fitting, and lacked even a spark of magic. Grimacing, he remembered the stranger witnessing the indignity and looked up again. The man took one step toward him before shaking his head. He offered no assistance, but his hands fisted, and his jaw was clenched hard enough to cause a tic.

The monitor in the room flickered to life with the image of Cabel's cousin, Alida. "Thank the blooms, you're awake. We've been so worried—"

"Why am I in a human hospital? Where are you?"

Before he could again attempt to sit up, the man was in his space. Cabel's eyes closed to relish the images of silvery snow that served to quiet his mind once more. The familiar scent of pine was mixed with a new hint of earth and storms. As he sucked in another breath, he felt strong arms wrap around and lift him before the bed moved to meet his body. Having to bite back a whine when a fluffy pillow replaced those arms had Cabel opening his eyes and glaring. "What happened?"

"That's what we're trying to find out. Wait, you don't know either?" Alida exchanged a look with someone off-screen. "What's the last thing you remember?"

A spurt of panic attempted to grow, but Cabel stared at the stranger and pushed it aside. The man's green eyes never left his as Cabel took a deep breath. His magic again barely quivered inside him. Inclining his head slightly, he focused on Alida once more. Brief flashes of their shared lives brought few answers as he stared at his cousin. There was comfort in the old memories, but his heart still ached, and his magic remained hidden.

"Do you recall the Dragon mission?" Alida's hands were clasped in front of her, and her ears extended into points. "Can you remember that?"

The mention of Dragons brought a familiar snarl to his lips. A huff of laughter pulled Cabel's attention back to the human. The man could have shifter blood as his eyes were more cat-like than human.

Cabel discarded the thought immediately. He could feel no magic and the human's eyes were also red rimmed which would make the color more brilliant. The stranger's face realigned into a blank expression. Humans weren't aware of Dragons, *Agoen*, or even Faeries...at least, few humans were aware and with good reason. Mankind had a tendency to be flighty, clueless creatures in his experience. "As you are not a healer, you serve no purpose here. Perhaps you should excuse yourself."

The stranger had the audacity to grin at the order. "No, I don't think I should. I might be able to help."

"I find that highly unlikely. You—"

"Who are you talking to? If that's Doctor Grann, be nice, Cabel. He's extremely knowledgeable and Trucu Center is one of the best places for magical care too."

"There's no way he's a doctor," Cabel disagreed without looking away from the man. Another quick head-to-toe scan revealed the weapons he'd somehow missed previously – assuming the scruffy scabbard lined with rope was a weapon. It was the shimmer of magic just above the human's foot that demanded his attention. "Where did you get the weapon in your boot?"

The stranger's hand gripped the strap across his chest instead of reaching into his boot. The unknown weapon pulsed with more energy. Cabel breathed in deeply but could still only enjoy the wintery scent that included no magic.

"A friend gave it to me." A small smile tugged the man's lips upward.

"Why would they give up such a valuable prize? You stole it. Didn't you?" The *reweial* revealed itself with a bright glow when Cabel focused his own magic on it. The powerful Faerie blade was used to kill dragons and did not belong with a mere human. It was rare enough that he'd only seen two and one was hidden inside his home in *Agoen*. "Did you kill the Faerie that blade belonged to?"

Even the ghost of a smile disappeared as the man cleared his throat. "Yeah, you could say I did just that."

The door burst open, and the Wolverine returned with a doctor in a white lab coat. The murderous human slipped away before Cabel could even call his magic to detain him. Alida and the doctor started speaking at once.

"Who killed a fairy? Cabel, are you in danger—"

"We need to do a few tests. While magic is clearly the root of your injuries, there is obviously a physical component, and we need—"

"Quiet," Cabel spoke over both of them. He struggled to stand and managed to scowl at the medical personnel and his cousin. "Do either of you know the man who was just here?"

"I do."

A new voice before a new being joined them. Cabel could see the glow of power surrounding the man and his own magic rose briefly in response. A ripple of annoyance followed but he tamped that down to retain an impassive expression for their staring contest. "Who is he and who are you?"

"He is the one who will help you get your memory back." The air sparked around the man who smiled. "I am Zaniel."

"Flapping fairy wings," Alida interjected.

Ignoring his cousin, Cabel concentrated on Zaniel as memories floated just out of reach. The mysterious human also warranted a few stray thoughts until Cabel pulled his magic around him as a mantle. "How could a human help me? How did I lose my memories?"

"Powerful magic was involved which is why you need the human guide. Your magic is unstable currently which makes you dangerous to your kind and even other magical beings. The human will not be affected by your magical whims. Your memories can be returned as they were taken, but you must walk the path a second time. You must accept a gift freely given."

"Why do I need a guide?" Cabel continued to frown as he struggled to process the mysterious words. His heart again thudded at an annoyingly fast pace.

"The rogue Dragon you were hunting still lives in Karsia. While most believe everyone abandoned those lands during Purgatory, that is not true. Both humans and all manner of supernaturals inhabit Karsia. The human was born there and can keep you on the path of truth. He's the one who can get you home again."

The words evoked bright images of a lush garden with abundant red berries, a rickety wooden bridge over raging blue waters, and even an orange sky. Cabel tried to grasp the memories, but they flitted away too quickly. The need to see Karsia was stronger even than his homesickness for *Agoen*. "Fine, I'll go with the human."

"Take care. Magic does not judge the world as Faeries or even humans. It sees the truth and accepts it. Will you be able to do the same?"

Cabel released his grip on the bed rail to stand unaided at the insult to his honor. "Death before dishonor."

Zaniel's smile was wide. "Sometimes, even magic needs a second chance, Cabel Orlaith, and this season is a special time for humans. Maybe Christmas will bring you a gift you've been missing."

"I don't need a gift from humans," Cabel denied.

His words had no impact on Zaniel's smile. "You believe that in your head, but not your heart. Unfortunately for many, belief doesn't change truth."

Chapter 2

C abel closed the trunk with a thud that didn't drown out Alida's happy squeal. She completely ignored that he'd denied her claim that the legendary Dragon and Fairy lovers had lived and could live again. His head ached after a solid week in the human realm. It was too loud, too unruly. His cousin fit in a little too perfectly.

"I remember you reading the story of Jacek and Tanwen to me. I never believed it was real though. Nash is researching his family books, and there's artwork that Reid recognized—"

"That's the human brother who draws on people's bodies, correct?"

Alida snapped her mouth shut and narrowed her eyes. "You don't have to act like such a troll. You know very well who Reid is. He's a gifted tattoo artist and, if you bothered to listen to me, you'd know he's even better at injecting magic into his ink. He's helped any number of supernaturals."

He'd only meant to tease his cousin. Being born outside of *Agoen* had marked Alida as different in their world, a halfling to some despite the royal lineage they shared. He couldn't deny that he'd always had a soft spot for her. Even her bonds with the Debare brothers hadn't stopped him from protecting and aiding her...and her witches. He was also intrigued by the idea of the human helping magical beings. "Who taught him to do that?"

Twirling away, Alida answered her phone instead of answering his question. "I'm not changing my bet. We're going to have snow this year. Brianna mentioned it to Kaye who told Nash and..."

Amusement caused Alida's top wings to shiver into existence in the human realm. A snow globe appeared in her hand, but it wasn't the one

Cabel presented to her. It was the first gift he'd ever given her and one of the only one he'd ever given freely.

"She keeps your gift on her altar."

Relief at the words almost made Cabel relax. The voice delivering the news had him standing taller. The witch shouldn't have been able to sneak up on him. He turned to face the Debare brother he and Alida had discussed. "Reid."

The man grinned and crossed his arms over his chest. The short-sleeved shirt revealed an array of tattoos. A few glittered with the addition of magic. "Even injured, you appeared to have kept a wand shoved up your—"

"Reid," Alida interrupted with a frown for them both. "I should just let you both sling all the insults you want. I don't know why I try to make you get along."

Before Cabel could offer a defense, Reid crossed the room to hug Alida.

"Because you love us and are too good for your own good," Reid chastised lightly as he kissed her forehead. "Don't worry, I'm leaving to meet a client."

"You'll be at dinner tonight, right? Lian and Nash are experimenting again."

Alida chuckled and clasped her hands together; Reid rolled his eyes but nodded.

"A promise is a promise, so I'll be there."

Cabel watched them hug and exchange kisses before the witch nodded to him and walked away. He'd never understood Alida's comfort in the human realm, nor her love for her adopted human family. A light sizzle of magic had his ears popping and Alida fluttering to his side. A rolled-up parchment floated in the air in front of them. Cabel grabbed it before she could and felt the rush of power of energy. Only three words appeared on the pages. "Tropes Are Us is the bookstore, right? Do you know what this Zaniel is?"

Alida shook her head repeatedly. "No, but he's powerful. I've wanted to search the Court library but—"

"You should do that, and you should not be here anyway. If he's right and my magic is dangerous to others—"

"I'm fine for a short visit and you just want me in *Agoen* because you think it's safer. Lian and Reid have my back here whereas those at Court would rather stab me in the back. What else is on the pages?" Alida crossed her arms over her chest and her wings fluttered behind her.

He couldn't argue against her logic, but he had to try. "Only the bookstore name. Perhaps that was true in the past, but if the Dragons are making a power play, Court will be united and will offer more protection to you. Can the witches fight a Dragon?"

"Lian and Nash already have, and they won," Alida countered before giving in to a smug smile.

"This Nash is the gardener you spoke of?" Glancing in the mirror, he noted the red of his uniform was dulled by the human world. His long sword, shiny and bejeweled, rested at his hip. Depending upon one's power, two, four, six, or none of his wings would be visible. At Court, every Faerie understood his family lineage and personal victories as revealed by the brilliant colors and symbols. In this realm, only those with sufficient magic would see the truth of his power. Humans had no real magic to speak of, but they would understand he was a warrior.

"He's more than that and your prejudice is showing, Cousin."

The title gave him pause and Cabel turned slowly as the air grew heavy around him. It was rare he felt his cousin's ire in her magic, but now was the exception.

"Whoa, lighten up, Alida. He is your favorite cousin after all." The second Debare brother joined him. Unlike Reid, Lian wore a three-piece suit. He waved a hand, and, after a pop and sizzle, the air softened once more. "I've brought a couple of spell bags for your trip assuming there's room in one of your trunks. I'm definitely telling Nash about this when he complains I've overpacked for the next publicity tour."

"It was only four stops, and all were in Tellum and Pagosah. You do overpack and you know his trunks will stay in the *Nuem*." Alida's tone softened even as she shook her head. She even smiled at the witch before facing Cabel again. "I'd take the bags if I were you. Nash is an excellent **gardener**."

"Alida," Cabel called out as she turned away. Standing stiffly, he waited for her to look at him once more. "I'm sorry. Thank you for your help and for coming to see me. It is important to all of us that the Dragon threat be eliminated."

Her shoulders slumped before she raced forward for a quick, hard hug. She kept her hands on his chest even after pulling away. "I wish I'd known you were already searching for Dragons. We could have used that information."

"You know the Court hoards information as the Dragons hoard gold. I couldn't tell you. Rister hadn't even substantiated the rumors before sending me." Cabel reached into his pocket for the holly berries.

"Your mentor is a big ole bag of troll nuts," Alida complained before conjuring a creamy snack pop.

He focused his energy on the holly hidden in his pocket, but it felt almost as if his magic was hiding. The loss of power was more of a challenge than the loss of his memories, but he had to believe both would return. Cabel still needed to complete his original mission – duty required it above all else. Dragons gaining power in the human world would have repercussions in *Agoen* and he needed to protect his kind. The berries shifted into a thin, nearly translucent wand that heated in his hand. He tapped the trunks and watched as they disappeared. His connection to *Agoen* remained true and he stored his belongings in the shadow realm easily. "Technically, we still haven't confirmed Dragons are causing the trouble as I have no memory of the events."

"You're taking that much better than I would. I can't imagine losing my memories." Lian tugged on his vest and patted down his pocket for his phone. "I've gotta make a call."

Alida's smile grew wider as she stepped away from Cabel. "Love looks good on him."

"Is that why his magic has changed?" Cabel had known the witch brothers most of their lives. The change was too obvious to miss.

"Speaking of changes, your magic feels different. Is it the injury or something more?" Alida winced then blew out a harsh breath. "Sorry, you probably don't remember. Lian is right though. You are handling this well."

It was easier to devote his thoughts to the Dragon problem than to consider something as trivial as emotions. Cabel wasn't blind to that truth, but that didn't mean he had to enlighten his cousin. "A few months over a lifetime such as mine is not of concern. Finding the Dragon, even if it's for the second time, will still eliminate the most pressing problem."

"But you didn't eliminate the problem last time. Why would this time be any different? Aren't you worried about losing more than your memories?"

Pain sliced through Cabel's chest, and he lifted a hand to press against his body. There was no wound, but he could still feel it. He had lost something more than memories when he last fought the Dragon...if that was the danger he had faced and forgotten.

"Cabel? Maybe you shouldn't go alone. I know Zaniel is powerful, but I could go with you and even—"

"No, you will not go. I don't know what happened previously. I do know you being a target won't improve the situation." He opened his arms and Alida raced to hug him once more. It was a human gesture that he had always found he missed after spending time with her. Faeries didn't follow such customs. "I'll be fine, little Cousin."

"I should make you promise," Alida threatened.

She wouldn't though; Faerie promises could not be broken without death.

"I can promise I will do my best to return, and I'll keep in touch since you are aware of this trip. The *Omil* crystals will allow us to communicate. All will be as it is meant to be."

Her nose wrinkled at the adage neither of them had ever liked. Alida rubbed her face against his chest before pulling back. "All will be as you will make it be. Find the Dragon and get back here safely."

When she became uncharacteristically quiet, Cabel frowned. "What is it?"

"Grann doesn't think I should say something, but he doesn't know you as I do." Alida's skin shimmered and darkened to a vibrant pink as her ears lengthened to points. "You used a crystal to contact me. You were happy about something, but you didn't tell me what. You only said you'd tell me when we were together again, and we could celebrate. You even suggested we meet in Tellum instead of *Agoen*."

Her words brought no excitement or remembered explanation. Shaking his head made the hope dim in Alida's eyes. She nodded before her human form concealed her true identity once more.

"Okay then, let's get to the bookstore and get you on the road again."

Alida's tone was as bright as her smile, but Cabel could see the brittleness in both. He pulled her in for another hug. After she walked away, he folded the blank pages and slid them into a hidden pocket in his uniform.

Chapter 3

Standing in the bookstore, Cabel scanned the literary offerings by humans. The closest cover included a man holding a baby with a black wolf below them. The cover proclaimed it to be the latest by Ryder Zemar and the best one yet in his <u>Feral Love</u> series. Next to it was a pair of men surrounded by blue and green swirls with the name Zari Arielle proudly headlining the covers.

"The Lion's writing has improved since he found his Mate." Zaniel reached out to straighten the books with a wide smile. "Maybe I should say since he found his Muse."

"Fascinating." Cabel knew his tone implied otherwise and stared at the man. "I'd rather hear why you're the one who can help me."

"Trust is a funny thing. It can be earned and lost in a single heartbeat. Too little can bring pain but so can too much." Zaniel studied him for several seconds and then smiled. "Sometimes, it can even change a life which changes the world."

Cabel didn't respond to the challenge in the being's tone.

"And sometimes, we refuse to see the obvious truth." Zaniel chuckled at his own words.

"Where is the human? What is his name anyway? I'd rather not keep calling him the human?" Alida stood nearby with Lian Debare again next to her. The witch didn't seem thrilled to be next to Zaniel either.

Zaniel winked at Lian and rubbed his hands together. "Farren Jeffries rejected my plan and returned to Karsia."

Cabel bit back a curse even as a puff of smoke curled up from the ground. The human called Farren appeared crouching with a bloody blade in his hand. While mostly clean, his attire of dull brown and white still left much to be desired. The weapon was oddly shaped despite having served some purpose. It fairly reeked of death, but there was also a whisper of magic.

"Son of a banshee," Farren stood and pulled a bottle from his pocket to capture the drops of blood from his weapon. "You do understand that harpy has already killed an entire family, right?"

"You hunt magical creatures?" Cabel asked.

Farren cleaned his blade without looking away from it. "Yeah, I do."

"I won't have him as a guide. Humans have always killed first and I won't abide by that stupidity." Cabel ignored the human to glare at Zaniel. "I'll go alone and—"

"And you'll be killed," Farren finished with a frown of his own directed at Zaniel. The blade was hidden and his arms were crossed over his chest. He bared his teeth with another human curse before facing Cabel again. "Karsia has its own rules and if the Dragon lives then he's more dangerous than you know. Your Court has no authority in this realm. Is your mission worth your life?"

Cabel stood at his full height but couldn't look down upon the human who stood just as tall and held his gaze. "Humans have little understanding of honor. Please allow me to assure you that a mission to protect my people is worth my life."

"Then you'll need me, and we need to know where to go." Farren turned back on Cabel to face Zaniel. "Are you going to tell me—"

"I already told your Fairy," Zaniel shared the lie over the human.

Frowning at both, Cabel shook his head. "You have told me nothing—"

"I gave you the papers."

The magical being also interrupted Cabel causing Alida to speak up quickly.

"The pages were blank."

"Were they?"

The human rolled his eyes then focused on Cabel as he pulled out the blank parchments to prove Zaniel lied. His hands warmed as he unfolded them. The first page did include a map.

"Well?" Farren prompted impatiently as he adjusted the strap across his chest.

"There is a map," Cabel conceded. His cousin leapt to his side to see it as Zaniel chuckled. While Alida was enchanted by the magical show, he was annoyed. He did appreciate that Farren was also glaring.

"Care to tell me just where you'll dump us or—"

Zaniel's interruption took the form of a magical relocation. It was rare for Cabel to feel a stranger's energy to such a degree. If there weren't bonds of family or a battle, his kind stayed cloaked in only their magic. Most other supernaturals kept a respectful distance from Faeries in *Agoen*. Zaniel's energy felt heavy and carried an unfamiliar scent as it smothered Cabel's power. Time and space bent around them. Cabel tried not to fight the push even as he felt Farren's struggle. He gripped the human's shoulder and squeezed. Light flared and twisted around and through them before they were standing on solid earth once more.

The air settled on his skin with a thickness Cabel didn't appreciate. Overgrown trees towered above them creating a canopy of green. A rainbow of flowers dotted the landscape, and the roar of water filled the silence.

"At least he didn't dump us in the river."

Cabel felt the man's shoulder twitch and released him. "Do you know where we are?"

He refused to flinch as the human leaned into his space to read the map. When the human snorted a laugh, Cabel glanced down at the papers he still held. Two small figures looking suspiciously like them appeared on the map. Red dots marked a trail to end in an X before an animated dragon blew fire. The page burst into flames and disappeared leaving the remaining pages safe and still blank.

"Yeah, I know where we are and where we need to go."

Stepping away from the human, Cabel studied a large bloom emitting a soft green smoke. The smell was sweet and unassuming white flowers sprouted purple berries as he watched.

"It's not as bad as I feared. Just a couple days hike and the terrain isn't too unfriendly." Farren dropped his bag to the ground and opened it up.

"Why hike? I can get us there faster." Cabel placed his hand in his pocket for the holly berries, but the human's fingers gripped his forearm tightly. A memory of hands on his body flashed brightly enough to send a shaft of desire through Cabel. He might not remember the most recent time, but there were plenty of carnal experiences he did remember clearly. Unfortunately, the memory disappeared before he could place the former lover.

"No, magic is different here, wilder. What works in *Agoen* or even Tellum won't be the same in Karsia."

He watched those long fingers peel back one at a time before the human's hand hovered over Cabel's arm briefly. The man turned away to leave Cabel alone to process his words and the surprising need still coursing through his body. "How do you know how things work in *Agoen*? Did the Faerie you killed tell you?"

"Yeah."

The one-word answer made it easy to switch the heat in his blood to anger and Cabel embraced it. He removed his hand from his pocket intending to set the human straight. A green vine slithered around his wrist and tightened painfully. The same purple berries he'd watched grow moments before now burst in a flash of heat and pain against his skin. Ghoulish images flashed in his mind's eye in a blur of shadows before the screams pierced his consciousness. Swaying on his feet, Cabel called his magic but an army of skeletons arose to—

Blinking, Cabel scanned the scene. One vine pulled back quickly to hide in a forest of green. The section that had been wrapped around his arm shriveled into dust at his feet.

"Welcome to Karsia," Farren spoke from his side as he swung a curved blade through the air. "Ghost berries bring nightmares to life in your mind. I told you things are different here."

"How different?"

Farren sighed and started walking forward. "There's time for a quick history lesson before we reach the bridge if you care to hear about the peasants, Princeling."

His royal lineage did grant him the title of Prince along with various other ones, but Cabel recognized the insult easily enough. The greenery surrounding him seemed to edge closer though so he followed the human without responding. There would be time to reprimand the cocky human later.

"I'll take your silence as agreement." Farren's arm swung in a fluid rhythm as he continued forward without breaking his stride. The blade hissed softly as it cut through the thick greenery. The plants shuddered and moved further away as a foul stench permeated the air. "They don't like to be disturbed and the shifters find the smell even more overwhelming than you or me."

"What type of shifters live here?" Cabel had always found it ironic that the reveal of magic had pushed humans into such close quarters of city life with both shifters and witches. Magic in the human realm had been further weakened as a result.

The human plunged ahead following a trail Cabel couldn't see. "We have all kinds. Citylife didn't work for everyone, but some were caught between realms during the Big Bang."

"The Big Bang?" It was a term that Cabel associated with human scientists trying desperately to understand a past when they couldn't even understand their present.

"It's what we call that first schism as they said the earth cracking open was deafening. It opened portals to other realms in Karsia and the influx of magic split the earth. Our ancestors called it the heartlands but much of it was flat then. The first years of Purgatory created canyons, rivers, and mountains that divided the land. Most humans rushed to the cities for safety."

"But not your ancestors? They preferred this life of uncertainty and danger?" Cabel glanced up at the blue sky before turning to see the green surrounding them. There was nothing hospitable or welcoming about the area.

Farren stopped abruptly and faced him. "My ancestors preferred freedom to living in cages. They walled up the cities and forced people into labor all in the name of survival. They feared the land and preferred to let people die on both sides of the walls." His shoulders hunched before the human rolled them back and lifted his head. He didn't speak before turning away to walk forward again. "My family and others wanted to live."

Being familiar with the human facts of Purgatory didn't prepare Cabel for his guide's passion. Purgatory had been a time of uncertainty and death in *Agoen* too. The war with the Dragons had continued even as portals were ripped open exposing their secrets.

"I know Purgatory was difficult in *Agoen* too. Everyone suffered whether they had magic or not."

The man didn't turn around, but his words still reached Cabel. He found himself relaxing at the obvious empathy. "My cousin was born in this realm and has always been connected to it. Until her, I had little experience with humans in your current century. Time moves—"

"Differently in *Agoen*. It's less of a river and more of a whirlpool." This time the human faced him to complete the words. Vibrant green eyes sparkled as he stared at Cabel. "I don't understand how that works, but I have heard that one before."

"Did you hear it from the faerie you killed?" The words weren't as sharp as Cabel had intended. The human had admitted to killing one of his kind and didn't deserve any kindness. Before he could remind them both of that, the human nodded once and turned away.

"We all make mistakes and magic can't fix everything."

Cabel almost stumbled into the man when he stopped abruptly once more. A wooden bridge extended from the ground to sway above crashing waves of blue. It was a scene Cabel knew he'd already witnessed. Instead of dread or caution, his heart and magic raced together, yearning to cross the bridge.

"After you, Princeling."

Chapter 4

They had trekked for the rest of the day after crossing the bridge, but nothing looked familiar to Cabel. His human guide had sent a few looks his way that Cabel couldn't interpret and wouldn't waste time trying. The landscape was unlike anything he'd seen in the human realm or even in *Agoen*. Magic rippled through the air creating an annoying buzz that roused his own energy in a new way. Living in *Agoen*, he rarely even felt the presence of outside magic. The Old Ways were intertwined in every tree root and every creature – it simply was. With little magic, the human realm always felt paler though humans added fleeting color and noise. Karsia was much brighter, warmer, and louder than both. "It feels wild, free. Can you feel the power?"

Cabel realized he'd stopped to ask the question and that the human was several feet away. Farren was again studying him.

"I've heard that before." Farren shook his head and started walking again. His voice carried back to Cabel. "What is magic like in *Agoen*?"

He had to think back before the most recent Dragon betrayals. "Calm, like a lake. This feels more like the ocean – moving, crashing, pulling." There was a shocking need to lift his arms and look up to the sky as he spun in a circle. Cabel pushed it aside with a frown.

"Karsia was calmer until the last decade. I didn't realize how different it was from the cities until last year. The changes are coming even faster now while the cities seem to be rebuilding slowly and more easily." Farren paused and gestured Cabel forward before pointing out into the distance.

Snow-capped mountains rose from the earth in the distance. Just below them was a valley with too-bright splashes of color moving together in a rippling, almost hypnotic dance. "Are those flowers?"

22

"They weren't here last month. We sent a scouting party, but they haven't returned. Communication is spotty here even by magical means." Farren pointed again, but this time to a small pile of rocks. "We used to mark paths and share information through specific designs. The forest changes too quickly to allow that anymore."

"No one in your village even knows where you are?" As a royal, Cabel was used to having eyes on him all the time. Finding privacy was a challenge. The idea of being completed alone wasn't as appealing as it'd once been. Breathing deeply, he pushed aside questions of his missing memories and instead focused on feeling his magic. There was only a hazy echo of his blood bonds to his kin. Being out of contact so completely chilled him to the bone.

"There have always been gaps in communication. Some families move throughout the year. Some have put down roots and built villages...though we call them towns. We're self-sufficient, but we do trade with others in Karsia and even in Novitum and Epizo."

Cabel tried to hide his surprise that the human was familiar with the western human lands. He couldn't ignore his own curiosity though. "Did Epizo fare better than Novitum during Purgatory?"

Shrugging, Farren returned to cutting a path forward. "If you ask Epizo, they claim they are more powerful as the shifters are in control and possess great magic. Novitum claims to be civilized, progressive, but also very human. They believe themself more powerful with less magic. Six one way, half dozen the other."

It was strange to hear so little concern for power or even the appearance of it. Even Alida, who loathed Court, understood and appreciated the necessity of the struggle. The humans Cabel had known were equally mesmerized by power. "You do not care where the true power lies?"

There was a brief pause in the progression before Farren surged forward. "I've found human and magical truths to be subjective at best. I prefer facts – that plant is edible, that one is poisonous. One will keep my people alive and the other will kill us. Those are the facts I live by. If it doesn't kill me..." The words trailed off as the human shrugged.

"You're only helping me to protect your people?"

Again, there was a stutter to the smooth swinging of the blade clearing their path. Cabel tried to read the truth in the man's aura, but his magic remained frustratingly weak.

"Yes."

For the next few minutes, there was only the sound of Farren's blade slicing through the thick greenery and their soft steps. The buzzing of Karsia's magic grew steadily louder.

"Get down!" After shouting the order, Farren dug blindly into his bag while scanning the sky and tree limbs above them.

"What are you doing?"

Farren launched his body through the air to tackle Cabel. He even managed to twist him, so Cabel landed on his stomach. "Stay down and cover your face."

The buzzing reached a feverish pitch before Cabel spotted the first of the large flying creatures. Segmented bodies identified them as insect shifters, but they were larger than any he'd ever seen. A sharp pain pierced his arm. Swinging wildly, his arm collided with one of their attackers. Another flash of pain – another swing. Rising, he reached for his sword, but Farren stopped the motion with a tight grip.

"Their blood is poisonous. Don't injure them. Just protect your head." Farren released him with a shove that almost sent Cabel to the ground again. The human started pulling something from his bag. One flying monster grabbed it. A brief tug of war ended with Farren flying through the air.

"Son of a banshee! I'm fine. I've got this."

Cabel ignored the words and focused on the battle. The creatures formed a dark cloud blocking the sun as they continued their assault. He reached instinctively for the holly berries. More stinging assaults had him fumbling to send sufficient magic to bring the wand forth.

A small explosion shook the ground but didn't scatter the creatures. Twin plumes of purple and yellow smoke twined in a quick dance until the coiling colors collided. Cabel turned his head away in time to see several creatures hitting the ground. The buzzing grew frantic as the others tried to flee. Several more fell before the sky was clear and blue again.

Cabel sagged against a tree then jerked upright as pain sliced through his back. Reaching a hand back, he noted the discolored bloodstain.

"Drink this." Farren shoved a bottle into his hand before drinking from his own. Purple bruises were already swelling to distort his face. Blood stained the man's shirt and dripped from his hands.

The golden liquid had a sweet scent. Cabel chose not to partake of the mysterious offering. He moved to the right to see one of the fallen creatures. Mummified, the black and yellow fuzz along its bodies had hardened into a sickly grey.

Hands pulled him roughly to his feet and Cabel turned his attention to a furious Farren.

"You could die here. Can you comprehend that? Even with your magic, you can be killed. When I tell you to do something, you do it. This isn't Court protocol or a wing-measuring contest. I tell you to run, you run. I tell you to hit the ground, you hit the ground. Got it?" Farren's green eyes were bright and hard.

"Are they shifters?" Cabel ignored the man's ramble and moved to stand over one of the bodies. "What kind of potion did you use?"

The human kicked a stone and turned with a fist ready to punch a tree. Instead, the guide took a shuddering breath and turned away. He picked up his bag and stuffed the fallen belongings back into it. "We've found a combination relying on yellow jessamine and mountain laurel effective. We trade a local witch for the potions and now I need more."

"And you blame that on me?"

Farren paused long enough to glare. "Yes."

Offering no other explanation, the man returned to gathering his possessions before standing. Cabel turned back to the closest body and knelt to examine it. He was pulled back before he could make contact with it.

"Even dead, they are still poisonous," Farren bit out the warning.

"To you perhaps," Cabel conceded. He studied the creature once more. "Do you know if there is a magical impact?"

"Do you want to test it out? You already look like you lost a fight."

It was only then Cabel noticed Farren's injuries had already healed significantly. Pain still radiated through his body with each beat of his heart. Focusing on it only served to make it more powerful. His skin rippled with a sudden itchiness.

"It will only get worse until you take the antidote." Now, Farren smirked – his face showed little evidence of the battle. "Your magic delayed the impact, but you have some nice bruises coloring that pretty face."

The compliment was tossed out haphazardly, but it gave Cabel pause. He kept his gaze locked on the human as he lifted the bottle to drink the potion. Thick and syrupy, it was even sweeter than the scent. The effect was instantaneous, and his pain disappeared.

"It's my job to keep you safe and I plan to do that," Farren offered quietly before turning away. "We should put some distance between us and the bodies. Those Melks have large colonies. I suspect these were just the scouts."

"They were scouting for flowers?" Cabel turned painlessly to scan for any flowers large enough to feed the bees.

"In a manner of speaking," Farren agreed. The smirk returned as he stared at Cabel for several seconds. "Melks are carnivores and feed on people, magical and human. They even devour other shifters."

Cabel knew his face reflected his surprise. Magic was usually seamlessly intertwined with nature – it didn't pervert or malign it. That was a job left to humans.

Chapter 5

With the pain a distant memory thanks to Farren's potion, Cabel conceded silently that the human was more knowledgeable than he'd assumed. The lands of Karsia also contained too many unknowns for Cabel. Despite the many dangers of court life, they were all things he'd always known and understood. Here, he would have to follow Farren if he didn't want to repeat whatever previous choices had robbed him of his memories and weakened his magic. The thought brought a rush of warmth too mild for anger. Frowning, he realized the idea wasn't as abhorrent as it should have been.

Farren dropped his bag, but he didn't sheath the blade. He made a quick circle around them as he scouted the surrounding area. "We'll camp here tonight."

Cabel scanned the space and found little to differentiate it from any other area they'd passed. A glance upward revealed a naturally darkening sky and no return of the creatures. "What did you call the creatures who attacked?"

"*Melkenai* is the formal name, but everybody says Melks. It's assumed they were bee shifters originally. The magical influx over the last decade has twisted the natural world even more than Purgatory." Farren stood and shook out two bed rolls. He placed one next to a boulder before removing his weapon once more. The strange shape of the tip now made sense as he used to chop down a small tree. "You know how it is with magic. Everyone keeps secrets. It's hard to know what is normal anymore."

"You've adjusted to the changes. That is a human gift. Magic moves more slowly in *Agoen* and not all adjust well." Cabel stood next to the boulder and watched the sparks when Farren started the fire. It was

27

tempting to use his magic or at least try. His wand had appeared easily in Tellum...when Alida had been close by and even in physical contact. He shook his head and found Farren grinning at him.

"Are you surprised humans have a gift you don't possess?"

"No," Cabel denied. It didn't seem like a smart strategy to share his thoughts, but it was surprisingly tempting to reveal his fears.

Farren barked a quick laugh and rolled his eyes. "I hope you lie better than that at Court. I've heard Faeri politics are deadly."

Cabel's mouth fell open before he could stop it. The human used the old pronunciation complete with a softer 'a' and an exaggerated roll of the 'r'. "Faeri? Humans don't usually understand the true term. Even my cousin says fairy though I blame the witches for that."

Running a hand through his hair, Farren remained quiet. There was a slight pink stain on his cheeks that intrigued Cabel.

"Why do you use the old term? How do you even know it?" Cabel couldn't stop from pressing for the truth. The human merely poked at the fire with the tip of his weapon.

It took a full minute before Cabel realized the truth Farren refused to share. The words escaped without his permission. "You cared about the Faeri you killed. She shared secrets and you honor her by using the old word. You must have loved her."

"Him," Farren corrected. He again set his brown hair to stand on end when he ran a hand through it before meeting Cabel's gaze. "I got too close to him and that's why he's gone."

Ice pierced his heart even as fire warmed his blood. The uncomfortable rush of conflicting feelings forced him to turn away from the human. Cabel collapsed onto the bedroom and pressed his back into the boulder. A rock poking his hip forced him to lie flat on his back to avoid looking at his guide. At the soft thud next to him, he turned to find a package wrapped in plain brown paper. A bottle filled with a pink liquid landed next to it.

"You should eat and drink something." Farren's mouth tightened into a thin line, but he didn't look away. "The magic here is corrupt and you're already been weakened, the smart choice seems to be to eat."

The words were caring; the tone was harsh. Cabel sniffed and felt his nose wrinkle at the strong herbal scent. Farren's chuckle pulled his attention away from the offering. The human's face had softened with yet another mood change. His green eyes sparkled with mirth.

"Yes, it's edible. We eat to survive here. It's not a formal ritual to show off one's wealth, bloodlines, and power."

Despite being a clear insult to Faeries, Cabel couldn't dispute the words. Unwrapping the brown square slowly, he also gave it several more sniffs.

"Just eat it, Princeling. You'll survive." Farren's smile was wide and friendly before he abruptly stood. "There's a stream just over there. I'm going to wash up."

The human's moods were more mercurial than a Phoenix feather and those flighty bits of magic were known for bursting into flames during potion-making. Lifting his head, Cabel ignored his guide's departure and took a small bite. There was an earthy taste with a sharp prick of an unknown spice. The taste wasn't unpleasant; however, the gritty feel against his tongue was. He wasted no time opening the bottle and washing it away.

There was little conversation even after Farren returned with wet hair, but the forest serenaded them with a cacophony of noises. Remembering the killer bees, Cabel again looked to the darkened sky. The stars were the brightest he'd ever seen, and he couldn't stop a gasp. While the wintery lands and skies of his home always shimmered, the dark sky caused the stars to sparkle in a different way. In that moment, he could understand why early humans were inspired to see figures, animals, and signs in the heavens.

The twinkling star calmed him as the forest around Cabel quietened into a few soft hoots and coos. He ignored the tossing and turning of his guide and allowed his magic to rest. Sleep wasn't the same for Faeries as humans but their meditative version of it was just as necessary.

Cabel drew on early memories of Alida visiting *Agoen*. He had been her guard and mentor. Coming from the human realm, his cousin had always been a bright star in her own right. He had encouraged her antics despite their family's disapproval. There were many good memories of her childhood to revisit for his rest.

A landscape of silver with only the dark green of holly and pine visible.

The sweet, heavy taste of their honeyed cream.

Alida's glowing eyes and bright laughter when he gave her a snow globe.

Calming as he drifted, Cabel started to count the multitude of sparkling stars in the sky...until they became emeralds. He remained in that restful space as the scene shifted completely.

Frothy blue water.

A hand gripping his.

Heat rushing through his body.

White flowers – green leaves – orange sky.

Waking, Cabel scanned the darkness before unlocking his muscles and sitting up. Either his memories were returning, or he'd had a dream. "Faeries don't dream."

The man across from him stirred on his bedroll but didn't awaken. Cabel cataloged every feature of his face revealed by the dancing flames. Facial hair was deemed unsightly in *Agoen*, but the scruff on Farren's face made Cabel's fingers itch to touch. His skin tingled as he could almost feel the soft hairs against his skin. The sudden desire to touch made less sense than his human guide. Faeries were known for their beauty and all his previous dalliances had been aesthetically pleasing. There was no logical reason he'd want a lowly human when their union would bring no magical boost to Cabel's power.

Logic didn't banish the yearning ache in his heart. Unwilling to close his eyes again, Cabel kept watch until the sky lightened and turned orange. The images from the night replayed in a quick, hazy succession once again. There was still no meaning behind them. That fact didn't stop his heart from pounding hard and fast.

Chapter 6

"You could've made coffee."

Cabel blinked at the grumbled words. While he'd studied the orange sky, Farren had awakened. The human moved with barely opened eyes to restart the fire and prepare the drink. Soft and sleep-rumpled, Farren fumbled the ingredients and cursed. Cabel smiled as he watched the show. Only after downing the first cup did his guide blink. Cabel took that sign as permission to speak. "Are you not a morning person?"

Farren almost dropped the cup when he stood abruptly. "Sorry, didn't sleep well. We should...let's get going." The human almost mumbled the last part before jumping up. He quickly put out the fire and re-packed the bags.

Stepping around him, Cabel silently offered his assistance. The sudden blush of pink on Farren's cheeks brought him up short. "Is something wrong?"

"Nope, nothin's wrong. We're burning daylight and should probably head out."

It took little time before Farren launched back into the jungle that seemed to have grown larger while they'd rested. Cabel paid more attention to the man's instructions as they traversed the strange land.

"Don't touch that. It won't kill you, but it'll hurt like a witch."

The white flower had appeared soft but closer inspection had revealed spikes.

"Hold your breath."

That order hadn't been quick enough as Cabel's foot had apparently disturbed what appeared to be a pile of fallen leaves. The foul stench

32

had still lingered for several minutes. Cabel stepped more carefully and nodded his appreciation to his guide's back.

"Wait..." A small pop followed by an explosion on their left. "Now, move."

The fire fizzled out quickly, but Cabel still stared without following. "How could you have known that was going to happen? You have no magical powers."

Pivoting in slow motion, Farren stared for several seconds. "No, I have no magical powers, but I'm also not an idiot. Stupidity will get you killed in Karsia. So will ego."

Cabel gave a single nod and again moved forward. The land made little sense, the man even less. When they finally rested, he relished the shady respite. He also found he could no longer contain his curiosity. "You mentioned sending a scouting party. Do you live nearby?"

Farren bit off another piece of the dry, tasteless bar he'd split with Cabel. A long drink of water was required before he tried to speak.

"There are several towns in Karsia." Farren's tone was slow and measured.

"Which one do you call home?" Cabel pressed for answers while searching the man's face for the truth.

Dusting off his hands, Farren stood and stretched. Cabel was still studying him even though he'd quickly suspected he wasn't going to get an answer. That silent denial didn't stop his gaze from frequently seeking his guide's visage.

Time inched by slowly without any words shared between them. They had covered a lot of land, so the next rest was a welcome one. Farren again seemingly chose a random location, but Cabel didn't argue. He even accepted herbal water and dried fruit from his guide. The strange heat in Karsia—

Cabel's foot landed and immediately sank. Stumbling forward, he was engulfed in golden sand to his hips. He instinctively reached for the holly berries in his pocket and sent a burst of magic only to feel the earth squeeze the air out of his lungs. The sand now reached his shoulders without any sign of releasing him.

"I'm going to toss this rope to you, and you will grab it." Farren had slammed his scabbard into the ground and was rapidly pulling the rope free. "Don't use any more magic. It only feeds on it and you that much faster. Now, catch this."

With one hand free, Cabel was able to grab the rope mid-air. He wrapped it around his wrist. "Now what?"

Farren left the scabbard jammed into the ground with the rope tethered to one end. Cabel was briefly distracted by the previously unnoticed prongs now anchoring the sheath into the earth while Farren pulled items from his bag. "What are you doing?"

The human ignored him to combine ingredients with steady hands. "Don't waste your breath."

The earth was swallowing him whole. Cabel nodded and tried to suck in more air. It was calming to watch Farren instead of the sand getting closer to his face. He was forced to spit sand to speak, "Faster would be good."

"I move faster, I screw it up and we both die."

"We wouldn't want that," Cabel agreed before shutting his mouth against the press of sand. He started to gather his magic to free himself. Regardless of his guide's advice, he started to gather his magic. The first glimmer of power had the earth tightening its grip until it started to crush him.

"Do not use your magic. I'm almost done." Farren didn't look at him to give that command.

An indelicate snort merely caused a spray of sand. The human finally stood as Cabel was forced to close his eyes. Before he did release any magic, the earth shuddered around him and enclosed him in darkness.

A flash of memories filled Cabel's mind: blue water, orange skies, and green eyes.

His lungs burned when fresh air flooded him. Farren opened his eyes to see only the golden sand trying to kill him. He reared back just as a hand pounded his back forcing a cough.

"Don't make my efforts pointless, Princeling. Breathe."

He sucked in a few deep gulps. "That would be easier if you'd stop hitting me." Cabel rolled onto his back and blinked at how close Farren leaned over him. The human's green eyes widened before he closed them and sat back. It wasn't a conscious choice, but Cabel clasped the hand closest to his body. Farren flinched and then his hand gripped Cabel's tightly for several seconds. The man pulled away leaving Cabel cold.

"Gotta gather these up. The blooms only last for a few minutes. I can preserve them, and they'll add power to several potions." Farren stumbled to his feet and kept his gaze locked on the ground. "That's why I told you not to use your power. The ground literally feeds on magical beings."

Cabel rolled to his feet. Even weak magically, his uniform stored enough magic to clean itself and him. It hadn't protected him against the threat though. "That is powerful magic. How did you stop it?"

Still pushing blooms into a red bag, Farren shrugged. "Trading. Everyone wants to live. Word had spread of a new threat, but I hadn't seen it, so I didn't recognize the danger signs."

"What are the signs?" Cabel knelt to scoop up flowers himself. He wasn't sure why he felt the need to keep the conversation going. It almost felt like a need to comfort which made less sense than the earth actively seeking his death.

"The ground had a shimmer. I should have paid more attention and—"

"Instead of trying to avoid my question," Cabel interrupted with a grin. Seeing pink stain the human's cheeks again made him fight back the need to touch once more. He could feel the hair covering a strong jaw, maybe even feel the heat of Farren's skin.

Farren met his gaze before smiling. "Now that's the skill a Princeling needs to survive in Faerie Court."

The use of the old word sent a new shaft of heat through Cabel. It wasn't only need but also jealousy. Farren had loved and killed one of his kind. Both ideas seemed equally ludicrous. It would take a special human to bond with a being like him. A human without magic ending a nearly immortal life was unlikely at best. Cabel's need to know the truth was also unusual, but he couldn't deny it. He wouldn't deny it to himself; he did bite the words back.

"We'll have to make a stop. The bag buys time, but it isn't a permanent solution."

Another sudden mood shift. The man who had calmly saved him and then blushed beautifully now appeared scared. Each facet of Farren's humanity revealed to Cabel fascinated him. He couldn't deny the need to protect the man. "Is the town unsafe?"

"For me? No. For you? Possibly." Farren stood tall with his smile in place once more. "Do you trust me to keep you safe, Princeling?"

"I do." Cabel wasn't sure who was more surprised by his answer – him or Farren.

They stayed quiet for the remainder of the hike and even bedded down with few words. Even with a tree at his back, he looked up once more. The sky was again spread out over him in a twinkling display. It wasn't the same as *Agoen*, but Cabel appreciated the beauty of the land...and his human guide. The fire played over the planes of Farren's face. Cabel's gaze lingered on plump pink lips.

He turned away and closed his eyes. The magic of the lands felt calmer than during the day. Even as Cabel watched though, a line of green vines inched closer. He saw the spark of magic force them back. Sitting up again, he scanned the space and realized the human had set up a magical barrier without him even noticing.

A quick glance proved Farren still slept. Cabel rose quietly and moved to the barrier that now pulsed softly in the darkness. He stretched a hand forward, but the protective boundary only hummed beneath his touch. Cabel's own magic fluttered at the contact and filled him with warmth and joy. He pulled back slowly with a sigh and again studied his mysterious human as he regained his seat.

Cabel's rest was filled with more brilliant images he couldn't remember...more images that left his heart aching for something other than *Agoen*.

Purple and white flowers.

Apples and emeralds.

Orange skies.

Blue water.

Chapter 7

Rubbing a hand over his chest, Cabel stared at the pink of the morning sky. Farren was standing at the edge of the border drinking his coffee. His hair was wet, and the light grey shirt clung to his still-damp body. Many questions filled Cabel's head, but he remained quiet. Too many urges required him to lock his body and magic in place while he took several breaths. The human still turned to meet his eyes.

"How do your Faeries politics explain the Dragons destroying humans in our world? Don't you have enough to fight about in *Agoen*?"

A spark of irritation heated Cabel's blood. "As if humans don't fight here."

"We do and you lord your superiority over us so why are you brought down by the same flaws?" Both of Farren's hands wrapped around the mug as he switched his attention to the dwindling fire. "Do you or do you not know what the Dragons plan could be?"

"I don't. As I didn't complete my mission last time, the Court has no new information. There are rumblings that the Dragons have turmoil within and gaining power in the human realm may determine the winner. It's imperative I find the Dragon here and get answers. Both of our worlds may depend on those truths." The words flowed easily until Cabel snapped his mouth shut. His guide had no idea how unusual it was for him to speak so freely.

Farren took a seat with a tired sigh. "I thought Dragons preferred orderly, solitary existences. How would chaos here help? How does killing humans bring power?"

Cabel blinked at more easy magical revelations from the man sitting across from him. The humans he'd met previously sought magic for power. Farren made no effort to even solicit his help even though Cabel would owe him a favor for his services. "We both seek the truth."

Farren looked up and gave him a slow nod before mumbling, "I'm just trying to protect the ones I love."

The words caused a new tension that plucked at Cabel's magic and reverberated through his body. However, he couldn't fully understand the reason for it. He could understand his body and magic seemed to agree with his guide.

"We should head out. The town isn't directly on our path."

Cabel found himself noting small quirks of his human as they continued their journey together. Farren walked faster the closer they got to the town. The smooth swing of his blade was interrupted by stutters and readjustments. He also glanced back at Cabel more frequently – sometimes, frowning, but other times, wearing a soft smile.

The sounds of people grew gradually louder; however, impending civilization only brought Farren's shoulders closer to his ears. Cabel fisted his hands to stop himself from reaching for the man. A series of small beeps signaled the return of phone service. Farren jumped before pulling out the small device and tapping quickly on it. He did this every few steps before stuffing the phone back into his bag with a mumbled curse. The man then cleared the path with more enthusiasm.

Following closely, Cabel's focus remained on Farren even when the small town came into view. More primitive than even Tellum, small buildings made mostly of wood were scattered across the barren land. A cabin with stained glass windows snagged his attention.

"Genie is a witch though some think she's a demon," Farren supplied the information.

Cabel lifted a brow but didn't reply. He did keep an eye on the cabin as they passed by it. "Is that why it's barren in town? Did she do that?"

Farren shook his head. "Supposedly deals were made in the beginning between witches and shifters to establish protected areas for all towns. The forest has gotten much closer over the last two years. One town completely disappeared."

Another glance showed a vibrant, orderly garden that fit neither the town's barrenness nor the wildness of the forest. Farren followed his gaze and smiled.

"That's Leina's place. Somehow, whatever is needed blooms even if it never has before. Sometimes, it never appears again either. We aren't sure what Leina is but she's powerful."

"Where does she live exactly?" Cabel stopped moving to study the garden from a safe distance.

Chuckling, Farren pointed to the garden. "Her cabin appears and disappears. She told me once that she is called by those in need and must help them."

"Called how?"

"I didn't ask, and you probably shouldn't either, Princeling. There are some even more powerful than you."

Moving with Farren, Cabel continued forward. His thoughts drifted back to Zaniel and whether the being could be trusted. The gifted blank pages remained in his pocket. Forcing his thoughts back to the present didn't bring any new information. Karsia still made no sense to him either. It was Cabel's turn to shake his head. "I do not understand why magic and nature are not living in harmony here or how that would benefit the Dragons." He hadn't meant to blurt out his thoughts, but Farren took the words in stride.

"I've been thinking about that too. Could it merely be a distraction? I hate to think of my people like that, but I know it's a supernatural arrogance thing. Could the Dragons be drawing Faeries out to make a move in *Agoen*?"

Cabel glared at the insult before processing the words. Farren's questions were not welcome, but the implications should have been obvious to Cabel from the beginning. "Humans have been used as pawns previously and the rules of *Agoen* do not apply here."

"Rules about Dragons and Faeries sharing power over *Agoen* with Phoenix and Gnome mediators? No one thought to put other realms out of play? For immortal beings, you aren't forward thinkers, are you?"

The teasing tone didn't change the truth of the words. "I'd like to have met your Faerie lover as he seems quite free with sharing our secrets."

A sudden burst of laughter had Cabel staring at Farren. The human's eyes danced, and his lips were pulled wide.

"I don't think you would have liked him. I didn't at first, but he grew on me." More chuckling accompanied Farren's words.

"You loved him despite your differences." It wasn't a question. Cabel could see both the joy and pain reflected in the sudden burst of colors surrounding his guide. His magic flared and the colors brightened before settling again into soft hues. It was the first time since he'd awakened without memories that Cabel felt his magic so strongly or had seen the world so clearly. With his Faeri vision, the human was even more beautiful despite the slight frown.

Farren struggled and turned away. "Maybe because of our differences. Who knows?"

A soft gold aura surrounded the man and Cabel couldn't look away from him. The words made no sense though. He had always chosen lovers based on magical compatibility. Every Faeri received a boost from a physical union with another Faeri. There was no need to fixate on one lover when so many possibilities were available. "You still love him."

His human's beauty didn't diminish with his grief. "I do."

A childish squeal interrupted their moment. After a brief flash of pain, Farren smiled and turned toward the noise. The sound seemed to have awakened the entire town as humans poured out of the buildings to converge on them. Cabel stiffened until he felt the heat of Farren's body pressed to his side.

"Relax, Princeling. It won't be as bad as dinner at *Kimnoas*."

The reference to a palace in *Agoen* did little to relax him. Farren had entirely too much knowledge for a human, but it didn't seem to prevent the man from treating Cabel with kindness and even risking his life to protect him.

"Farren, you're really back!" A small girl with dark curls threw herself against his guide's legs.

Pretending to stumble back, Farren pressed against Cabel briefly before lifting the girl high in his arms. "I am back, Lady Lilly. You appear to have grown enough for three summers."

She hugged him close and whispered, "I missed you."

Cabel heard the fervent words even over the noise of the crowd. He also saw Farren's aura flutter as the man held the child even tighter.

"Lillyane, I told you to wait for us." A petite woman with a child on her hip scolded with a smile.

"Do you really have *Gathos*? Can I see them?" A younger boy snuck through the throng to tug on Farren's pants.

"Earth flowers aren't real."

"They are so—"

"That's enough, boys."

More voices spoke over one another as many reached out to hug or shake Farren's hand. Colorful auras lit Cabel's visions even as his ears rang with the noise. Farren pressed lightly against his side and the world quieted a bit. Cabel kept his place at his human's side during the extended greetings.

CABEL WAS STILL BY Farren's side when they sat down for a meal in the largest of the town's buildings. Adults and children alike ate together. It was a human custom Cabel had witnessed previously, but it felt new, different somehow. He froze in place when a child stood on unsteady legs and clutched his thigh. Big blue eyes studied him too seriously for such a small body.

"Zoe is thriving as you see, but I think she missed you." The same woman who chastised Lilly spoke again. "You should spend some time with her."

It took a moment for Cabel to understand the stranger was speaking to Farren. He glanced from the speaker to his guide and then to the child. "You have a child? A family?"

"He rescued her from a chimera attack. The monster burned down most of the village before Farren got there, but he saved Zoe. Right, Mama?" Lilly beamed with pride as she shared the news.

"There are chimeras here too?" Cabel hadn't heard of *Trikas* in years. He turned to get Farren's response, but many others jumped in quickly.

"Those beasts are powerful and a single one can destroy a town."

"Magic has brought us nothin' but monsters."

"It's brought us medicine too. The scales Farren brought back saved old man Hesiod."

It was clearly a long-standing argument and many quickly chimed in. There was much more magic in Karsia than Cabel had realized if their words were true. Farren though remained quiet except for a few whispers with Lilly's mother. Cabel focused on their exchange to eavesdrop easily.

"Do you really think it will be different this time?"

"It has to be. I'll make sure of it." There was an urgency in Farren's tone that Cabel hadn't heard previously.

"At what cost? You almost died last time and—"

"I have to try," Farren interrupted her. He squeezed her hand then smiled. "If we do nothing, nothing changes."

"Not all change is good. I'd hate to see you hurt again." Tears welled in the woman's eyes.

"And not all second chances change the future. They definitely don't change the past." Farren released her hand and scanned the room.

"Farren, maybe—"

"No, that's enough, Nina. We're not talking about this."

Chapter 8

A fter the shared meal, Farren gave several bags to various adults. He accepted multiple offerings and stuffed them in his bag. There were also shared updates on other humans Cabel did not know. He did recognize the flicker of sadness on his guide's face when deaths were revealed.

"Do you know what happened?" Farren studied a bottle before adding it to his bag.

"The White Wolf still makes journeys through here and he brings a lot of information. There's only rumors."

"We did have only rumors of the killing earth too, but now Farren has confirmed it exists."

More revelations of the changes and dangers in their world were revealed. There were also more goods exchanged as they bartered not for power, but to survive. Cabel tried to picture Faeries allowing such free exchanges without deals but couldn't. A tiny fist thumped against his elbow guards. Lilly looked up at him with a smile.

"Mister Cabel, why is your clothing so bright?" The small girl's smile revealed a missing tooth.

Human children often saw magic adults missed so her question wasn't surprising. "It is infused with fairy magic."

Her face lit up as she giggled and nodded. "And that's because you're a fairy with magical powers, right?"

Cabel had no time to answer the child.

"May I touch the red?" Lilly's hand was outstretched but she didn't touch him.

He knelt in the dirt in front of her. "The red symbolizes my f—"

"Family, I remember!" The girl's hand trembled in the air before landing over Cabel's heart. "I love my family. Do you miss yours?"

The child reminded him of Alida and Cabel's magic pulsed with power. A too-large snow globe appeared in the child's hands, and he quickly used his to help her hold the gift. It didn't look as he'd intended. Instead of *Agoen* in shimmering silver, the sky was blue despite the fluttering white snow and a giant pine tree decorated in the human style filled the sphere. There were even brightly wrapped presents beneath the tree.

Lilly's delighted gasp was easily heard over the deafening silence of the adults.

"Thank you, Mister Cabel. I'll keep it forever and ever."

There was no time to warn the child about expressing gratitude to his kind. She scampered off to show her mom her new treasure.

"Yes, it is beautiful. Walk carefully lest you drop it." The woman's smile turned quizzical as she faced Farren, not Cabel. "And you still think things will be different this time?"

His human guide stared at him with wide eyes before jerking to the side and walking away. When Cabel turned to follow him, Lilly's mother grabbed his arm. She let go quickly and bit her lip.

"I'm sorry for touching you without permission, sir. This is all...very strange." She glanced up and peered at him with narrowed eyes.

Cabel wasn't sure what she was looking for, but he didn't move away or speak.

Swallowing hard, the woman dropped her gaze. "I'm Nina. Thank you for the gift. Take this with you, please." She pressed a small tissue-wrapped square into his hands and then practically ran after her daughter.

With neither Farren nor Nina present, the crowd dispersed quickly without making direct eye contact with Cabel. He was left standing alone in the empty street. There was no choice to make as to his direction and within minutes he found Farren sitting next to a well.

"I require nothing from the child. There's no debt to repay." Cabel watched as Farren's shoulders dropped at his words. Words of apology coated his tongue with sticky sweetness, but his guide spoke first.

"I appreciate that. Lilly is a good kid. They are good people only wanting to live their lives in peace."

Nodding along, Cabel thought he understood. "They are why you are helping me. They are why you fight deadly creatures, to save them, to save children like Zoe. I will make a deal with you, Farren—"

"No, no deals," Farren spoke over him with a snarl. He shook his head repeatedly and paced in a small circle. "No. No magic, no deals. We find the Dragon and end this. That will protect Zoe, Lilly, and all the others."

Cabel couldn't help but stare following the outburst. "Why would you not want magical aid? You just traded for potions and amulets to protect you. You carry a Faeri weapon. Why would you not want my help?"

Running a hand through his hair, Farren turned slowly to face him. "There are some things magic can't fix."

THE WORDS REPEATED in Cabel's mind with each step away from Farren's town. There was still too much he didn't understand about his guide. Neither that truth nor the man's rejection should hurt, but Cabel again rubbed a hand over his heart. The yearning for something fluttered inside him. "I apologize if the gift was inappropriate for Lilly. I meant to give her a globe similar to Alida's, but magic is very different here."

Farren was again required to clear a path for them, and his blade paused before moving once more. He didn't speak so Cabel tried again.

"I can send something more practical. Healing herbs perhaps? Maybe something they can use to barter or—"

"Your gift will give Lilly hope and that's priceless. There is no need for a replacement. Let the child believe in a bright future as long as possible."

"Farren of Karsia, do you not believe in a bright future?" He might not want to help his guide, but Cabel couldn't deny the need to try to do so. He just needed to actually understand the man enough to offer appropriate aid.

This time, Farren stopped and turned to face him. "I believe life is too often about pain and suffering and anyone who claims differently is lying."

"Karsia is dangerous," Cabel conceded with a nod. He glanced around already knowing what he'd see. "Your lands are also beautiful. Removing the Dragon's corruption will protect your people and mine. I failed last time, but I will not make the same mistakes again."

The man winced and turned away. "Maybe it's just a human thing to repeat our mistakes then. I hope you're right and we defeat the Dragon for good."

They journeyed together in silence for the remainder of the day. Cabel's curiosity burned inside him while leaving him cold and achy. The sky seemed to darken with his mood, but they didn't slow down again until Farren claimed they would camp in another randomly selected location.

When his guide moved to guard their space, Cabel watched him carefully. Farren reached into his boot while his lips moved silently. Drops of blood landed on the earth to draw the magical boundary protecting them; his human was hurting himself to protect them both. Cabel's magic hummed and he directed it to reach for the spell. Jumping back when sparks flew, Farren glanced back at him and froze in place.

"My magic will boost your protective spell. As you are protecting both of us, it only seems fair that I contribute." Cabel didn't wait for an acknowledgement but instead unrolled both sleeping bags for their use. When he looked up again, he found Farren working on the fire.

The first pink sparks revealed more magical tools Cabel had previously overlooked.

Apparently, it was only his magic the man rejected.

Chapter 9

It wasn't dreams that pulled Cabel from his rest. It was punishing pellets of frozen water slipping between the canopy of leaves overhead.

"Son of a banshee," Farren grumbled as he climbed from the bedroll. Scanning the sky and then the lands, he cursed again, "Can't we catch a break?"

Cold seeped through his uniform and Cabel looked down. He should have been protected unless... "It's a magical storm."

"Thanks, Princeling, I got that news bulletin. The temperature in Karsia has stayed hot since Purgatory. We don't get freezing rain here." A shiver running through Farren's body interrupted his rant.

"We have to find cover before you freeze." Cabel moved to touch the magical boundary and channeled his energy through it. A bubble appeared over them protecting them from the shower. "It won't last, but it will provide some assistance."

Even as he spoke a drop of water landed on Farren's forehead. The man swiped at it and nodded. "Yeah, let's go."

Cabel grabbed one of Farren's bags as the guide struggled to hold his weapon and light. The temptation to use more magic was almost irresistible but he couldn't risk harming the man. His magic was closer to the surface now. That didn't mean it was no longer dangerous.

They slipped and slid for over an hour. The exertion kept them warm, but Cabel could see how Farren's arm slowed. Staying back several feet, he called his magic to improve his eyesight. A quick scan allowed him to see the cave and he pushed his magic down again. "To the right, there's shelter."

Farren didn't question him as he trudged in that direction. It wasn't long before they saw the cave.

"Wanna bet on anyone or anything else using it?" Farren still moved toward the entrance with a grimace.

Stopping the man with a hand on his arm, Cabel stepped slightly in front of him. "No bets. Wait." Another release of magic illuminated the empty cave in full detail and set the weapon in Farren's boot aglow. Cabel ignored it and stepped inside first. The distance didn't last long as his guide followed closely behind them.

"Not much space, but it's dry." Farren knelt to pile rocks together and immediately started a fire. The pink flames lit the space and filled it with warmth and the scent of honey.

Closing his eyes to breathe in deeply, Cabel opened them to find a half-dressed Farren. Golden skin pebbled over rippling muscles as his guide continued his hurried striptease.

"You might want to do the same. The fire is limited without actual wood, but it's already drying out the bedrolls."

He hadn't even noticed their sleeping bags positioned around the dancing flames. Cabel blinked and glanced once more at the man standing before him. Removing his briefs, Farren knelt to feel the bedrolls. It was impossible for Cabel to look away from the man's ass...even as he wished he'd turn around to reveal the front of his body.

"Stop being a creeper staring at me and get warm." Farren didn't turn around to provide the order. The chuckle belied any harshness of the words.

"I'm not cold." The last words ended his teeth chattering. Cabel shuddered against the cold fighting the heat pooled low in his body. Without offering any explanation, he worked with trembling hands to remove his uniform without magic.

Wrapped in his bedding, Farren stood and turned to him. Cabel froze in place when the man smiled and reached for him.

"Here, let me help. Without magic, you Faeries are practically big babies." Again, the tone was soft and fond despite the word choice. Farren quickly found and released the hidden clasps.

Warmth from the fire rushed over Cabel's skin. He couldn't look away from Farren's eyes or move to continue undressing. The next shiver through Cabel had little to do with the temperature. Despite the lack of true magic in the human realm, time seemed to stop as they stared at each other. Magic sizzled inside him and sent the fire leaping higher in response. Farren pulled away abruptly.

"You can handle the rest. I'll brew some tea to help. Maybe we can catch a few more hours of sleep after that." Keeping his back to Cabel, Farren worked on the tea and set other items out from his bag to dry.

He grasped for words to fill the silence and distract himself. "How will your town handle this change? Will they be okay?"

"They'll survive. It's what we know how to do, what we have to do."

Cabel stopped his movements at the words which seemed in response to something other than his question. Farren had also stopped moving, but his head was dropped low enough for his chin to rest on his chest. He pulled in several deep breaths and then looked up to continue working.

"If Dragons don't like cold, why would he corrupt the weather to create this?"

Moving slowly again, Cabel undressed and wrapped the bedding around himself. "Magic is supposed to live in harmony with nature. There's been too much corruption to control it."

"You tapped into yours easily enough without killing us."

"I did, didn't I?" Cabel replayed the scenes in his mind. While his memories were still missing, he had easily manipulated his magic to do his bidding. First, he'd tapped into the protective boundary and then again when he'd searched for safety. He turned slowly to study Farren. There was an obvious answer, but it made no sense. The mystery surrounding his guide deepened and pulled Cabel closer. He stepped directly behind the man without choosing to do so.

Pivoting quickly, Farren flinched back. He avoided eye contact as he spoke, "I'm ready to sleep."

Cabel found his discomfort amusing. "What about the tea you promised?"

"I didn't promise." Heading snapping up to deliver the response, Farren glared at him. "Fix your own tea, Princeling."

SWIRLING MISTS OF *Agoen*, cool and crisp.

The scent of pines, sharp and familiar.

Sweet honey and tart berries bursting with flavor.

Cabel allowed the memories to drag him closer to his magic, closer to oblivion. Warmth flooded his body and soothed the ache in his chest.

A child's laugh.

Budding blooms in a rainbow of colors.

Softness and warmth.

Taut muscles and heat.

New scenes played out in excruciating details but too quickly. Both *Agoen* and Karsia served as backdrops to the action.

Farren's lips against his own.

The feel of soft hairs sliding through his fingers.

Clenching hands, a rough scrape against his thighs, gasping breaths.

The coiling pressure of pleasure ready to burst.

Jerking awake, Cabel could feel the need in his magic and his body. His hips pushed forward seeking friction...and found it in the form of Farren's naked hip. In his rest, he'd somehow wrapped himself around his guide. Green eyes with wide pupils stared at him.

"Sorry, just a dream." Cabel fought the need to relive the images in his mind.

"Faeries don't dream."

The whispered denial had him meeting Farren's eyes and Cabel couldn't look away. He couldn't close the distance either. There was no denying his human was aesthetically pleasing. There was no hardship in staring at his strong features. However, something stopped Cabel from seeking closer contact. "Karsia must be corrupting my magic."

Though Cabel had whispered the excuse, Farren flinched away.

Now the yearning in Cabel's heart twisted painfully. Shaking his head, he sat up. "No, I only meant—"

"No explanation needed." Turning onto his side, the human gave his back to Cabel.

Before he could stop himself, Cabel watched his hand hover in the air, almost touching the broad expanse of vulnerable skin. Almost.

"Yeah, you've probably been corrupted. Might want to keep a distance then, Princeling."

Pulling his hand back, Cabel nodded though Farren couldn't see his agreement. He gathered the material around himself and twisted to face away from the temptation. His guide continued to speak.

"We'll be close to the Dragon's lair tomorrow. One more night and we can go our separate ways."

His heart again ached at Farren's words. He had failed the last time he'd been in Karsia and couldn't afford to fail again. Those thoughts didn't stop his heart from aching for...something more with his second chance.

Cabel waited until Farren's breath was slow and steady before facing him again. The man was lying on his back with the fire highlighting his beauty. It was the memory of the man with his people that Cabel chose to dwell upon though. There was no push for power or even a recital of all he'd done to protect them on their journey. Farren had even downplayed past efforts such as saving Zoe. He was fighting to protect those he loved just as he'd claimed.

It wasn't truth or honor that motivated the man. Farren was all about love and that made Cabel's heart race as his magic burst forth to light the cave. He pulled back his power when his human stirred. Cabel smiled when the man curled onto his side. A soft golden aura was the only magical color remaining and it surrounded his human.

Cabel tucked the dried bedroll more tightly against his human and brushed the soft hair back from his face. "I promise to protect you, Farren of Karsia."

The words flowed easily and brought Cabel surprising comfort as he settled back to watch over the man as he slept.

Chapter 10

The bitter scent of coffee pulled Cabel from a rest he didn't remember seeking. He jerked up to find Farren watching him with a blank face. His human's gaze flicked down once, and Cabel realized he was still nude while Farren was completely clothed. Licking his lips, Farren looked away. Hot desire pooled low in Cabel's body even as he too turned away. A pulse of his magic had him covered once more...and also reignited the fire just as Farren reached for the crumbled rocks.

"What the fox?! You couldn't have waited until I wasn't touching that?" Farren's hands were covered in angry red welts.

All of Cabel's strength was required to stop his magic from trying to heal the man and his mouth from uttering an apology that wasn't wanted. Farren dug into his bag and scooped out a green cream from a small canister. He rubbed his palms together while still grumbling.

"It's time to go."

Those were the last words spoken between them for several hours. Karsia demanded their attention as Farren stopped frequently to clip new flowers and note changes in the land. Cabel could feel his magic rising up in answer to the pressure building around them. If the Dragon wasn't alive and terrorizing the lands, then something worse had taken its place.

Instead of a steady pulsing beat of magic and nature together, the world erupted around them in a tumultuous and unfamiliar clash of energy. Cabel's ears popped and his fingertips tingled. Even Farren winced and rubbed his temples as the pressure built. The return of Karsia's heat and humidity didn't help either. It was more than enough to make Cabel wish for a cooling breeze or even a freezing rain.

"I've never felt anything like this. Is it Dragon magic?" Farren paused in a small, barren patch of land.

"They do prefer to play in lakes of fire and quartz, but even their lands in *Agoen* are more comfortable than this." Sweat dripped down Cabel's face and he wiped it away again. Much like the freezing rain, the magic calling forth the heat was too much for his uniform to fight. He noted Farren making a similar motion. The man's short-sleeved shirt clung to his body in a translucent film. His hair stuck out in spikes from frequent tugs by impatient hands. A dark flush stained his face even as his skin glistened under the harsh sun.

Teeth, sharp and playful.

Kisses, light and teasing.

Hands linked together as pleasure crested.

Shaking the images away, Cabel cursed under his breath. Whatever magic was at work, it was torture seeing a life he wouldn't have. Love wasn't an option, but he had a mission and a promise to fulfill. "Let's keep moving."

Farren wiped at the sweat dampening his face and neck. "Alright, alright. I'm moving."

Cabel walked back over to him and reached slowly for the weapon. Neither looked away as Farren released his grip with a nod. Swinging the modified sword, Cabel was surprised by the weight of it.

"Yeah, yeah, I know. It's rough and heavy while yours is a true sword meant for battle." There was exasperation in the tone but also amusement. Farren rolled his eyes and rested his hands against the scabbard's strap. "Out here, it needs to do more than just slice dragon scales or pierce rival Faeri's armor."

Bringing the blade to a stop in front of him, Cabel took a moment to press and prod to release the multiple tools hidden within the weapon. "The rope and prongs on your sheath saved my life already. It is clever to use your weapon as you do. There's a purity and beauty in its usefulness too."

Snorting a laugh, Farren shook his head. "I guess you are a good one to talk about beauty. I just know it keeps me alive."

Cabel didn't acknowledge the words or the brief flash of pain that accompanied them. He walked past Farren to continue clearing the path. While he couldn't read the land as his guide could and there was no trail, Cabel felt the growing pull of magic.

"I guess I don't need to ask if you know which way to go," Farren grumbled.

Another few hours passed as they shared the task of clearing their way. Next to a small stream, the land settled as if a quiet bubble of protection insulated it from the Karsia's current mayhem. Both paused and took several breaths. Cabel scanned the area while Farren dropped his bag and pulled the scabbard off.

"Someone has protected this space." It wasn't a magic he recognized which made Cabel wary.

"I'd guess Zaniel."

Pivoting, he saw Farren holding a paperback with the name Ryder Zemar written at the bottom. This time, it was a golden lion positioned underneath the image of two men and a baby. "I still don't know if he's friend or foe."

"We can add a layer of our own protection. Maybe clear a bit more space so we aren't completely inside his magic." Farren tossed the book to the ground to reach for his weapon and Cabel handed it off.

They extended the protective bubble and blessed it with their shared efforts. The potion ingredients came from others, but the tools Farren used were his and magic respected them. Cabel could feel their energies blend and watched the reds and greens settle easily in a boundary of their choosing.

"Will killing the Dragon reverse the corruption?" Farren spoke only after they had shared a meal. The man was stretched out staring at the night sky above them.

Cabel couldn't help but focus on the aura of magic gathered around his guide's feet. The *reweial* still remained hidden as neither of them mentioned it. Releasing a soft sigh, he looked at the sky and answered, "I don't know."

Farren twisted onto his side and met his gaze before focusing on the fire needed only to protect them and light their camp. The magical flames offered no heat as they burned the wood they'd gathered.

"Potions and spells can be reversed, but whatever magic has been worked here has intertwined with nature. That is the way of magic in *Agoen*, but the human realm has separated the energies over the centuries. Killing the Dragon will stop additional corruption while we look for a way to cleanse the lands."

"We? You planning to stick around, Princeling?" Farren's lips twisted into a teasing smile, but the man didn't look away from the fire and a blush brightened his cheeks.

When he'd awakened in the hospital, Cabel had yearned to return home. His heart still ached, but he knew it wasn't for his ancestral lands. The fleeting images haunting him served to make him want a different life. It should have been a frightening realization. Instead, it felt comfortable, even familiar. He shook his head and studied the fire too. "I think there's more to do, more I'm meant to do. Honor demands I see this through."

Farren's nod was abrupt before he turned to lie on his back again. "Honor, of course."

The half-lie was easier than voicing the truth. Parts of Cabel were still missing, and his journey wasn't over. Honor was part of it, but so was need.

"There's more to life than duty."

At Farren's quiet words, anger heated Cabel's blood. "Do you not want to see Lilly again as you promised? What of the babe you rescued? We both still have jobs to do. There are duties that also bring happiness."

There was a ring of truth to his words that froze Cabel's anger. Alida spoke often of seeking happiness for herself and others. It was the first time Cabel had understood her dreams. It was also becoming easier to appreciate her love of the human realm and those humans she considered family.

Laughter of a man, not a child.

Comfortable embraces.

A steady heartbeat.

Happiness.

Locked in a battle with the memories or dreams in his mind, Cabel almost missed Farren's next words.

"And there are duties that break hearts."

Chapter 11

Cabel used magic to get the coffee going before Farren had awakened. It was worth the risk to see green eyes widen before crinkling with delight. The appreciative sigh sent a shaft of desire through Cabel's body. A desire not only for pleasure but also happiness – shared pleasure. His human was sleep rumpled but no less beautiful bathed in the beams of the sunrise and his own golden aura.

"We should reach the mountain this afternoon."

Blinking at the words, Cabel nodded automatically. He both wanted the journey over and to linger in the cave with Farren. There were no words to explain his conflicting thoughts to himself and certainly not to his human.

"And that will be the end."

With those words, Farren moved quickly to prepare for the day. Cabel was still struggling and unwilling to move forward yet. Their little camp was a tranquil spot protected from magical whims. He was still sitting on a rock by the stream when Farren started packing their bedrolls.

"What is your town called?"

Farren paused for a second before closing his bag with a snarl. "What does it matter? Did the presence of humans offend your honor?"

He hadn't expected such a response to an innocent question. Cabel moved to the stream and splashed water on his face instead of responding. He then took several breaths and faced his guide once more. "I supplied the coffee. Shouldn't you provide breakfast?"

Much like with the quicksand, Cabel realized his misstep too late.

"Because everything is a deal? Honor requires reciprocity?" Farren ripped his bag open and tossed something through the air. It landed with a splat in the water at Cabel's feet. "Son of a banshee."

Picking up the water-soaked package before Farren could, Cabel straightened and met the human's gaze. "Are you okay? Did you receive bad news in town?"

Farren watched him unwrap the bar and take a bite. Cabel tried not to grimace at the rough texture and earthy scent. His guide's lips twitched before Farren tossed his head back with a laugh. Though he didn't understand the mood change, Cabel enjoyed the man's amusement.

"Okay, Princeling, you can stop pretending you like the food. There's a berry bush by the waterfall. Let's grab those."

Cabel followed quickly and even stepped further when Farren knelt to pluck plump red berries. The sound of the waterfall was loud, but it wasn't within their protected boundary. He turned back in time to see the succulent fruit Farren held up. Automatically, his mouth opened to bite into the treat his human offered from his own hand. Juice spurted out causing Farren to smile before he popped the remaining piece into his own mouth.

They spent the next minutes picking fruit for breakfast and to carry as a future snack. The interlude was enjoyable, but Cabel found the food tasted better from Farren's fingers. His guide was no longer angry and that would have to be enough for now.

"Come on, Princeling. We have a Dragon to defeat."

For once, Cabel was grateful for his human's moodiness when Farren frowned again. He couldn't stop the niggling hope that there would be time for him to adjust as Farren had.

Stepping back into Karsia's heat had both groaning. After only an hour of traveling, Cabel noted Farren's increased discomfort heralded an increased moodiness.

"What the fox is happening? I'd like the land to stay the same for just one day. That's all I'm askin' for." The human plucked several spiny seed balls from his shirt and flung them aside.

"Have you heard the story of Jacek and Tanwen?" Cabel smiled at the brief memory of asking Alida that every night whenever she'd visited *Agoen*. He couldn't help but think of the small child waiting for Farren back in town. "Perhaps, it's a story Zoe will appreciate?"

His guide blinked several times, sipped from a water bottle, and then gave him a wide, beautiful smile. "You should probably tell it to me then."

It took several seconds of staring at his human before Cabel nodded and forced his attention onto the path ahead of them. "Yes, I probably should."

He still took the time to drink from and return the offered water bottle. "Our *Palachi* have shared this story for generations. I even—"

"*Palachi*? What does that mean?" Farren continued to clear the path without breaking his stride.

"Instead of supernatural or immortal, we use the word *Palachi* for our Ancestors. It translates roughly to old soul." Cabel enjoyed sharing the explanation, but he still grinned before schooling his face to a blank mask. "Are you going to interrupt whenever I use a word you do not know? If so, I fear it will take much longer to tell the tale."

Now, Farren's movements stuttered before he spun to face Cabel. Whatever he read there had him rolling his eyes and facing forward once more. "Funny, Princeling. Are there going to be a lot of Faeri secrets I don't know?"

Cabel chuckled and stepped quickly to follow his human. "Perhaps. How am I supposed to know what you already know?"

Another pause before Farren shook his head. "Good point. Should I be the one telling a story then?"

"I would like to hear more about Karsia and the creatures you've met…good and bad," Cabel blurted out the request quickly.

The rhythmic cutting continued for long enough that Cabel feared he'd misstepped once again. He opened his mouth as he heard Farren start to speak.

"You might be able to shed some light on a new story. We have a man who most people call White Wolf. He is a shifter and that's not strange. He's not the only one who stops in to trade with us." Farren paused only to step over a large fallen tree and offer a hand to Cabel before continuing. "He's been helping people leave Epizo because they are in danger. He's told a story of ancient Hunters called Orions and the Wolves who fight them are—"

"Romans," Cabel completed the sentence with a nod. When his guide turned to face him, Cabel took the blade and started to lead them forward. "That is an old tale that I have heard. Supposedly, some men used magic to call for help from angels while others made a deal with demons. Both claim to have uniquely powerful magic for humans."

Farren's amused snort made Cabel smile. He even paused to look back at his human.

"We've now moved from magic to angels and demons. You don't find that hard to believe?"

Shrugging, Cabel started forward once more. "I once thought our tale of Jacek and Tanwen was a myth but even now my cousin is researching it as truth." He paused as he remembered the changes in Tellum that Alida had shared. Their worlds were changing and there was still much to learn.

"Could our White Wolf have some unusual magic then? He's been calm and quiet from all accounts. I haven't seen the people he's transporting, but Nina always sneaks in extra food as they appear malnourished."

Cabel wasn't surprised to hear the concern without judgment nor that Farren's people had provided help without payment. "The people he's helping leave are being hunted by the Orions?"

"I don't know as I haven't spoken to him personally. We weren't even sure he was telling the truth."

"Perhaps Alida can help you locate some he's taken to Novitum to ensure they are faring better now? I'll need to send her a message soon and can make that request."

"Not one but two Faeries helping poor little humans without any expectation of payment?"

It was Cabel's turn to pivot around to see amusement dancing in Farren's green eyes despite his carefully blank expression. He rolled his eyes before laughing. "Funny, human. I believe it's your turn to work again."

Their conversation provided a distraction from the miserable weather; however, it didn't stop Cabel from noting how quickly the heat weakened his guide. The additional stops extended their journey and he saw no reason not to appreciate that strategy.

Chapter 12

Their journey did have to end, but finding the Dragon's lair was still only the next step. The small cabin was not what Cabel had expected. There was no gold, no jewels – there was an abundance of human gadgets and trinkets. He almost smiled at the thought that Alida would have been perfectly comfortable there...if it was a room in a Tellum apartment and not a cabin almost merged into the mountain deep in Karsia.

"Gotta say this is disappointing," Farren commented.

"There must be a passage to the real lair. As the beast isn't here, we should search for it. Let's split up." Before Cabel could move away and use his magic, Farren grabbed his arm.

"You know the Dragon would defend itself against your magic. Let's stick together and search the human way."

Nodding, Cabel moved to follow Farren to the first room.

"Don't pout, Princeling."

"Faeries don't pout," Cabel argued. He caught his reflection in the hall mirror and tightened his mouth into a straight line.

They made quick work of the few other rooms, but the library was overflowing with most of the possessions. Bookshelves lined all the walls and were crammed with books, glass bottles, and what appeared to be wooden boxes. The large desk and chairs were covered with fabrics and papers. There were multiple plants hanging from the ceiling and perched precariously on top of the rows of books.

"The passage must be hidden in here." Cabel barely resisted the urge to use his magic.

"There's a lot of stuff here." Farren plucked a book off a shelf and stumbled back when the wall moved away from him. A blast of cool air rustled the pages on the desk. After only a second, he leaned forward to peer past the hidden door. When he turned back to Cabel, Farren was grinning. "Found it."

As soon as he grabbed the man's arm, Farren shook his head. "Nope, the Dragon is employing human methods to hide so no magical senses crap. He clearly didn't consider a Faeri lowering himself to work with a human so I'm no threat to him."

Cabel released his grip with a nod. He hadn't considered Farren as much either in the beginning. He had been wrong, and the Dragon would be too. "Certainly an error in judgment on the Dragon's part."

Farren stepped through the passage. A fear twisted like a Karsia vine around Cabel's heart, both piercing and constrictive.

'Take care, magic does not judge the world as Faeries or even humans. It sees the truth and accepts it. Will you be able to do the same?'

Zaniel's words repeated clearly in Cabel's mind, but there was no obvious truth to see. Like his magic, the truth remained hidden from him. He had to leap forward to catch up as Farren plunged fearlessly ahead. The man separated the firestone from his weapon handle and sparked it to life to light their way.

"Proceed with caution. You are not immortal."

"Technically, neither are you. You're just an Old Soul who is a bit tougher."

Lips twitching at Farren's casual dismissal, Cabel still tried to reply sternly. "More than a bit."

They crept quietly through twisted stone tunnels. The temperature had warmed with each step, but it was still nothing compared to the heat of Karsia. It was easy to understand why a Dragon would enjoy the heat, but the instability of Karsia would be more dangerous for a Dragon than a Faeri. A well-protected lair would help negate that worry which made it more important to protect the space.

The passage suddenly widened into a large chamber lit by flickering lights. His magic surfaced easily and set the grey stone to light in brilliant technicolor. Cabel again grabbed Farren's arm. He pulled hard enough that the human's back collided with his chest.

"What the..." Farren whispered the words without completing the sentence. He glanced over his shoulder at Cabel.

Briefly distracted by Farren's muscular body and bright eyes. Cabel managed to shake his head and then lifted a hand. His magic shot forward to trigger the trap before Farren did. The heat from the blast of fire had Farren pushing harder into Cabel's body. His free hand landed on his human's hip...only to steady him, of course.

"Okay, maybe your Faerie senses can help, but be careful and keep the power on low." Farren continued forward once more.

Twisting and turning, the stone tunnel continued toward the heart of the mountain. The temperature increased just past Cabel's comfort level, but his magic adjusted his uniform accordingly. Though it remained hidden, his magic was more easily available, and that truth helped Cabel relax despite the upcoming battle. His sword pulsed with energy and there was an answering glow from Farren's boot. His human's multipurpose tool remained dull and quiet. Cabel still gave a slight nod as the weapon had cleared their path and had even saved his life. Farren tugged on the strap that cut across his body and then pulled his shirt away from his body. The heat of the Dragon's lair might be uncomfortable, but it did nothing to detract from the man's beauty.

Shaking his head, Cabel focused on the danger ahead. He again pulled Farren back and allowed his magic to spring another trap. With his human resting against him, they watched the spikes pierce the stone wall.

Farren leaned to the right to touch one. "That would have hurt."

"You're welcome," Cabel prompted with a straight face.

Winking at him, Farren then held his gaze and smiled. "Thank you, Princeling."

Instead of moving forward, Farren plucked a small chisel from the hilt of his weapon. "Dragon magic must have some use, right?"

"Yes but handle it with care." Cabel conjured a protected cloth and held it out, waiting.

The spike fell into the cloth once Farren freed it from the wall. A rotten stench had them both leaning away. Cabel wrapped it quickly and pushed it toward Farren.

"Thanks, I think." Farren pulled out a bag and stuffed the wrapped spike into it. "Should I get more?"

A rumble sounded before the ground shuddered under their feet.

"Maybe on the way out?" Cabel didn't voice his concerns that they might not make it out.

Chuckling, Farren nodded. "I like that you're entertaining the idea that we live through this. Okay, let's go beard the lion in his den."

"A Dragon is much more dangerous than a lion and a beard is irrelevant," Cabel couldn't resist pointing out. The answering snort from his human made him smile. He pressed a hand against Farren's back to push him ahead, but also kept it there as they walked forward.

Cabel's magic flared before he could pull it back. Farren moved with him to hide at the edge of the opening. Farren extinguished his firestone, but lights continued to flicker along the stone wall. Taking a deep breath, the stench of fire and sulfur burned Cabel's nostrils. They'd not only reached the heart of the lair, but they'd also found the Dragon. He started to ease his magic out when Farren grabbed his arm and shook his head.

He followed the human back several yards, but Cabel kept his attention on the creature. Farren knelt to pull a small bag from his backpack. The scent of pine clung to the crushed yellow and orange blossoms. "I'll sneak around to place lines at any other entrance."

"How could you know to use jasmine and witch hazel?" Cabel took another breath to relish the familiar scents.

Farren kept his attention on his hands as he wrapped a length of twisted pine needles and sap around his wrists. "If you're gonna take on a Dragon, it helps to be prepared."

"That still doesn't explain how—" Cabel tried again.

"Do you want to defeat it or not? The pine will protect me, and I can block the escape routes. You'll still have to battle it again. The Dragon won't care that I'm here, but you'll be..." Voice trembling at the end, Farren snapped his mouth shut and gritted his teeth.

Memories of another battle teased Cabel's mind with fire, pain, and fear. The scenes were jumbled, messy, and unfamiliar – he knew the battle hadn't taken place in *Agoen* which meant it was one of his lost memories. A new spike of fear pierced his heart causing it to both race and ache. Rubbing a hand over his chest, Cabel focused his attention on Farren. "I won't lose this time. I'll finish our mission."

Cabel sealed the promise with a kiss. Farren was warm and pliant in his arms and his lips molded to Cabel's with ease. The ache in his heart was overwhelmed by warmth, affection, trust, and need. Such emotions could be detrimental during battle, but Cabel brushed his mouth over Farren's once more. He eased back to find they had both wrapped their arms around the other. The fact that Farren's breath was fast and choppy made Cabel smile until he realized his heart thudded loudly in his chest. He cupped his human's cheek and leaned in for another kiss...

Pebbles and dust sprayed them as the stone above shook and crumbled. A great roar sounded before a blast of fire knocked them back.

White hot heat – sharp pain.

Chapter 13

C abel helped Farren stand then pushed him to the side as another rush of fire targeted them. The Dragon had destroyed part of its own lair to expose them. There was no time to talk – Cabel had to fight.

Farren stumbled from the strength of Cabel's push and then started back toward him.

"No, stick to the plan. I must face the Dragon again to fix this." The holly berries heated in his hand as they formed a glistening silver wand. Magic sparked along Cabel's skin in a joyous rush even if he still wasn't at full power and his wings remained hidden. One quick slice sent a blast of icy air that pushed the Dragon back. "Go now, *Imisi*!"

There was only time to see Farren nod before the Dragon attacked again with another scorching assault. Wind whipped through the chamber as their magic collided with thunderous noise. Pressure built quickly only to explode whenever a strike landed.

Fire and ice.

Crackling. Sizzling.

His uniform heated as it absorbed another blow and forced Cabel back. The temperature rose several more degrees past balmy to blistering. He scanned the cavern but barely noted the clutter that far exceeded the mess in the library. Farren wasn't even visible amidst the boxes, shelves, baskets, and books. However, Cabel could feel his human's racing heart. His magic swirled around him before he directed a wintery blast toward the Dragon.

Pine trees and snow.

Red scales sparkled as the creature reared back from the assault. Human lore noted the blazing breath, but not the spiked wings that literally fanned the flames. Twin strikes flashed toward him and Farren.

The stone heated at his back as Cabel listened for the shuddering inhale. He waited until the first tremble to call his magic out. A quick glance proved Farren still lived, and Cabel took a quick breath of his own. He then stood with a raised arm.

A spiral slice of his wand released a glacial arrow straight toward the beast's heart. The Dragon's breath caught in its chest. The upward flick sent a twisting green vine to ensnare, but the Dragon recovered enough to flick its tail and block the strike.

A black cloud gathered above them; the ground cracked and splintered under them.

Cabel sliced through the soot just as blue fire knocked him back. A second orange flame flicked his wand from his hand. The Dragon sucked in a breath while Cabel struggled to move away from the suffocating heat. His wand disappeared under the smothering magic, and he was unable to call it back.

Sulfur and lava.

Fire and death.

A frigid gust allowed him to suck in cooling air as the hilt of an ancient Faeri blade slammed into his hand. *His* blade. The magical symbols glowed even as a protective shield buffeted the newest wave of fire away. His fingers wrapped around the weapon as he met Farren's gaze. His human's hand was still outstretched. There was no longer a glow of magic from his boot, but a golden aura surrounding him quivered. The blade in Cabel's hands vibrated and warmed against his skin.

Swinging the blade, he regained his feet. He coughed as he sucked in air to clear his vision. Magic flowed from his uniform and into his body, cool and refreshing. Cabel focused the flow on the charred stone surrounding them. He even gathered power from the magical boundaries Farren had placed and continued to swirl the energy.

Cabel faced the Dragon once more and met its black gaze. With a quick puff of chilly air and a flick of his blade, yellow jasmine sprung up from every crevice and the Dragon snarled.

Rain fell as the dark cloud lightened to a silver glow. The drops of water hardened into icy spears. Now roaring, the Dragon shuddered and swayed.

Spiky green vines slithered forward to ensnare the beast. Pink bell-like flowers bloomed with a cooling wind. The blade sparkled in Cabel's hand. He crossed the space and plunged into the beast's chest. It wasn't a killing blow...yet.

A drop of Dragon blood slid down the blade to land on a snowy white flower. Light burst overhead as brilliant as the Karsia sky.

The entire world froze around him. Even a drop of Dragon blood poised along the blade fought gravity to remain hanging in the air. The red Dragon was immobilized mid-snarl.

Realizing his magic had again brought unintended consequences, Cabel turned to Farren. Even his human's heart was stilled by his magic. Racing to his side, Cabel clutched his outstretched hand.

Memories and magic returned to Cabel between one heartbeat and the next. The force of both stole his breath. He was staring at the man he'd given his heart to...twice.

Almost all of the returning memories focused on Farren and the human's golden aura pulsed softly in response.

Frothy blue water surrounding him – a familiar hand gripping his.

Heat rushing through Cabel's body as Farren drew flush against his bare skin.

A bouquet of white flowers offered by his human lover.

An orange sky embracing the setting sun as they embraced each other.

Shared secrets, fears, and hopes.

Hope. Trust.

Words not only of lust but also of love and laughter.

Imisi...other half.

Promises of a happily-ever-after, promises of forever.

He had even taken Farren to *Agoen*. Purple and white flowers had decorated the large bed they'd shared. A gift of emeralds and apples as his lover's green eyes were ever-changing and always beautiful. Pink fire had warmed them when they'd swam in the midnight blue lake next to his home.

Cabel was the Faeri who had shared magical secrets, and it was his blade Farren carried. He was the one Farren had loved once upon a time. But now...

In that frozen moment of time, it wasn't only a journey of love with Farren that crystallized so brightly in Cabel's mind and heart. He also remembered the first time they had faced the Dragon together.

That battle had been in the heat of the Karsia jungle. He'd thought he was prepared, had thought his sword and blade would certainly bring victory. The Dragon had been distracted by the trap they'd set – rubies, sapphires, and gold. Cabel had spilled the creature's blood and wounded it grievously, but the Dragon had been close to Farren and had lashed out with claws and fire to destroy him.

He'd sent his *reweial* to his lover and Cabel had imbued it with sufficient magic for his human to wield it on his own. It had been a desperate act to protect Farren and he'd miscalculated the impact of Karsia's corruption on his efforts. Farren's face, streaked with blood and eyes wide, was Cabel's last memory before pain and darkness. He had tried to protect his lover but had ended up hurting them both.

There was no way to deny he was at fault. He had been distracted during the battle, cocky about his power, so sure of his victory.

His mistakes had cost him Farren.

'Magic does not judge the world as Faeries or even humans. It sees the truth and accepts it. Will you be able to do the same?'

He wouldn't lie to Farren again and he wouldn't fail. He had to save Farren, even from himself.

Chapter 14

His magic rippled as the Dragon fought through the frozen enchantment. Before the creature could free itself, Cabel heated Farren's mind and heart. Green eyes blinked dazedly before sharpening with fear.

"Worry not, *Imisi*. I want you to hear the truth from the Dragon's mouth, but he cannot know you are awake. I will protect you." Cabel yearned to reach out and touch, to offer comfort, but he could not. There was another truth he had to accept along with his own failures – Farren had hidden the truth of their shared past. His human's eyes widened and then he blinked once.

Swallowing back more promises, Cabel turned to face the Dragon as the creature's own magic started to free it. A quick slice of his palm and a handful of jasmine blooms allowed Cabel to draw a circle around the beast. It would unfreeze, but it wouldn't be able to leave or call for help telepathically from its own kind. He added another spell that would force a change to its human form. With a roar and a puff of blue smoke, a human woman stood before them. Red scales became a fitted red dress fully covering her arms and legs. Straight, inky black hair framed sharp features with glowing black eyes.

"I did not expect to face you again, Fairy Prince."

That answered his first question. She remembered the battle, so it was only his memory that had been impacted by his magical choices. "Nor I you, but here we stand. I have questions and you will answer truthfully."

Even in her human form, the Dragon released an unnatural hiss. "And you will release me? You might as well try again to kill me. I won't let you destroy this realm too."

Cabel again felt his love's heart beating with his own and smiled. "You are not the one destroying Karsia, are you?"

She blinked wide, yellow-gold eyes and frowned. "You will not believe me, but I have no reason to hurt humans. We are seeking balance and peace. It is your kind who lies and plots in cold darkness."

"Tell me how you came to be here, Dragon."

Another hiss before she paced the small trap. When she faced him again, she glared. "I do not understand why you are asking these questions now. Last time you were only too happy to kill me."

"It does not matter why. Speak the truth and I will free you." Farren bowed slightly and watched the Dragon's mouth fall open. "I promise to release you from this trap without further harm if you tell me the truth."

A shake of her head sent a curtain of hair over her face. When she pushed it away, her eyes shifted from black to yellow and back to black again. "You know the story as I do. With Jacek and Tanwen sleeping, *Agoen* has been in turmoil for too long. It is your kind who are preying upon the opportunity for more chaos and blood. It is your kind who released the corruption into this realm. We have been trying to save humans from Fairy wrath and greed."

Alida also believed the myth was true, but Cabel had placed little importance on a love story recited to children. He had focused on battle plans and royal intrigue. Another mistake. "Are there other Dragons in the human realm?"

She released a brittle laugh. "Of course, we are the ones known for fiery moods, passion, and speed. Unlike your frozen nature, we are willing to get dirty and even enjoy it. The human realm is more hospitable to us than *Agoen*."

A quick glance showed Farren splitting his attention between Cabel and the Dragon. His human's heart still beat inside him, steady and strong, as part of their magical bond now restored. Cabel continued to scan the space before staring at the female once again. He couldn't afford more mistakes and she had knowledge he lacked. Snarling, she spat the next words at him.

"We won't give up our ancestors' lands to you, snowfly. You do not deserve to live in peace and prosperity."

Cabel waved a hand through the air, disregarding her tirade. "I know there's a Dragon in Tellum too. What about the other lands?"

Fire sparked as she growled. "Do you think you can defeat us all?"

He needed to realign the players on the board to correct his mistake. "If magic was intentionally released to cause chaos, it was meant to draw you out. To weaken and distract you."

Another fiery scoff. "Weaken me? You couldn't defeat me last time and you haven't won yet either. More blood will be spilled. You might consider human deaths a distraction, but we do not."

"You misunderstand me. *I* don't want to weaken you." If he was putting the pieces together correctly this time, he would need not just human help but Dragons' assistance too. "I'm hoping to work with you."

She paused to study him and then looked at Farren before laughing. "It's not me you want to work with, it's him. I knew there was something between you last time."

Cabel moved to block her view even as he fully reversed the spell to free Farren. His human coughed and then swallowed hard before moving to stand next to him. He couldn't help but place a hand on Farren's back and smile at him.

"Aww, how sweet." The Dragon's lips curled up with a half-snarl.

"You're lucky to be alive. I'd try to play nice." Farren faced her with a glare of his own.

It was a difficult choice. Cabel wanted to both kiss his man for his bravery and also protect him from foolishly angering a Dragon. He focused on the woman instead. "Do you have any plan to reverse the corruption?"

Farren never looked away from the Dragon. "Do you have any evidence that it's Faeri instead of Dragon magic?"

She stepped to the edge of the circle and crossed her arms over her chest. "I'll need to be released to answer both questions. We have proof and a plan."

A hand latched onto his arm. Cabel leaned closer to Farren but didn't look away from the threat. His human closed the remaining distance to whisper against his ear.

"You can't release her. She'll kill you."

"*She* has better senses than you, human. Your Faeri is more of a threat to you than I am."

Farren bristled at her interruption and Cabel stroked a hand down his back. It wasn't the first time he'd completed that action and memories and need stirred at his motion. "I need the proof she has."

"Then we'll search the lair ourselves," Farren agreed loudly.

The Dragon tossed her head back to laugh. "Don't know many Dragons, do you? This isn't my only lair. Do you have months to find and search all of them? How many of your kind will die while you do so?"

His human grimaced as he scanned the cluttered space.

"We must come to an agreement, Dragon. I'm willing to make a blood promise if you are." Cabel held his *reweial* aloft, ready to draw blood.

Chapter 15

"**I** do not like this plan," Farren repeated his complaint.

Grinning at his love, Cabel winked before facing the Dragon. "As you know, if anyone breaks their word, they die."

"Yes, yes. My blood will freeze and yours will boil. If you seek to re-assure your lover, then talk to him. I don't need the ritual explained to me." She rolled her eyes and blew out a sigh. "You should call me Phyllia and I will need your name, Fairy."

Farren gritted his teeth and spun on his heel. He only took two steps before returning to Cabel's side.

"I am Cabel, and this is Farren. My blood protects him but does not bind him to our deal." Cabel held her gaze until she nodded. He sliced through his palm and repeated his vow. "If you speak the truth about your plan to stop the corruption in this realm and your proof of Faeri responsibility for the corruption, I will release you without harm or further obligation."

The Dragon extended a claw and used it to cut her other hand. "I will speak the truth about our plan to stop the corruption in this realm and our proof of Faeri responsibility for the corruption. I make this vow of my own free will and accept death for breaking it."

She held up her hand just inside the boundary. Cabel stepped close and lifted his hand to repeat the final portion. "I make this vow of my own free will and accept death for breaking it."

When they clasped hands, the cavern shook with a thunderous boom. Red and blue sparked before forming a purple knot over their joined hands. A sudden breeze dispersed the knot in a shower of glowing embers.

"Death before dishonor," Cabel intoned at the same time as Phyllia before they released their hands.

Tossing her hair back over her shoulder, the Dragon smirked at Farren before looking at Cabel again. "You'll need to release the trap before I can get the proof."

Farren paced behind him, but Cabel kept his attention on Phyllia. Karsia was Farren's specialty; supernatural politics was Cabel's unfortunately. He drew his sword and held it aloft before sending the weapon to rest in the shadow realm as a show of trust. "Of course, allow me."

The Dragon strutted across her lair with a sensuous grace; Farren continued to glare at her.

"You'll recognize these as fairy stones, yes?" She turned one of the many wooden chests toward them and opened the lid. "You can come closer, little human. I won't bite too hard."

Cabel crossed the room to inspect her proof. After only a second, he felt Farren pressed against his back as he peered over Cabel's shoulder.

"I've seen those before. How is that proof?"

Waiting until Phyllia nodded, Cabel picked up a handful of the cross-shaped stones in a variety of colors and sizes. It wasn't only the shapes that confirmed her words. His Faeri senses brightened the colors and revealed the symbols.

"I believe your legend claims they were tears of grief," Phyllia prompted.

Closing his hand around the stones, he didn't confirm her words. "May I keep these?"

Her gaze flicked from Farren then back to Cabel. "Sure, clearly, we have enough for our purposes."

"And what are your purposes?" Farren demanded.

She released another laugh before turning away. "You may not believe me, but protecting humans is one of them. There's a cleansing ceremony we've been performing. Grinding the stones to dust provides the last potion ingredient to counteract the corruption."

A sudden flash of heat against his chest had Cabel pulling the pages from the hidden pocket. Zaniel's bookstore name was no longer the only words visible. He scanned the page and recognized the ritual. "The *Therpulia?*"

"Yes, we have our scales, Gnome stones, and Phoenix feathers. It's not ideal working without gifted fairy dust, but we knew your kind would not help undo your destructive efforts."

Farren pressed a hand against his back, but Cabel knew what he had to do. "We can do the ritual together."

It took little time to prepare for the ceremony, but that also meant Cabel had no time to explain it privately to Farren. His returned memories brought little comfort as past him apparently hadn't revealed much in that area. His human had seen his wings because Cabel had chosen to show them. Another memory teased him...

FLASHBACK

Standing under the waterfall, Cabel extended his wings and relished his lover's low groan of appreciation.

"The wings cover your ass which is a crying shame," Farren called out from his place stretched out on a flat rock.

Cabel heard the telltale splash as his human approached. His wings extended to greet the man and Farren's first brush along the appendages had him groaning.

"However, these...they, your wings" -Farren paused to chuckle as one wing brushed against his face- "are beyond stunning. I can't believe you've hidden them until now."

"Do you want me to tell you what they mean? The colors?" Cabel still found it disconcerting how easily his human managed to fluster him even after they'd been sexually intimate for months. He'd once foolishly underestimated humans and Farren, in particular. Now, Cabel was excited about sharing his life with his human. He'd even reached out to tease Alida with the big changes in his life...she was really the only one who would appreciate and support his new plan.

Hands slipped through the wings to trace Cabel's stomach. Farren pressed into his back and wrapped his arms securely around Cabel's waist. His wings folded back to envelope the human causing Farren to chuckle.

"I do want to hear all the secret symbolism and then I'd like to give round two a try. Maybe something mid-air?" Farren hummed happily and even rocked his hips forward.

"You do have a...what did you call it earlier? A wing kink?"

His lover's husky laughter sounded right by Cabel's ear. He closed his eyes to savor the joy the man continued to bring him.

"I think it's just a you kink, Princeling. We have other creatures with wings, and they never got me excited. 'Course, their wings weren't nearly as sexy as yours." Farren nuzzled his neck as the wings almost vibrated against them. "Yeah, you're gonna have to fess up with those secrets quickly...and then round two."

Farren moved them inside the small cave, behind the wave of water. Once he'd found a comfortable rock seat, he pulled Cabel to straddle his lap. His wings flared behind them and Farren watched with dilated eyes while he gripped Cabel's hips. The golden aura surrounding his lover pulsed with a bright warmth.

"Your wings really are different from the shifters." Still staring, Farren moved one hand to stroke the nearest one.

"Time for a history lesson," Cabel began before pausing as his human chuckled.

"I really would have done better in school if you'd been my teacher." Farren leaned forward to flick his tongue across one of Cabel's nipples.

It was a familiar conversation since they'd crossed the line to lovers, but Cabel still enjoyed the lighthearted teasing. In *Agoen*, it was his bloodline and magic that others appreciated. Farren simply appreciated him.

"They do look different in *Agoen*, but yes, they are also different from beings in this realm. Shifters have connections to animals so any of their wings reflect that bond. We'd be most similar to Dragons, but their fire connection changes their wings." Pausing, Cabel allowed his wings to wrap around them both. When Farren shivered at the silky, soft touch, he smiled. "For you, they are soft and welcoming."

"Yeah, I don't need another demonstration of their blade-like appearance. I guess with your winter preference, it'd be more like deadly icicles." Farren pressed a kiss into one wing and then turned and repeated the process with the other. "Tell me about the colors."

Humming happily at the gentle touches, Cabel leaned forward to rest more fully against his lover. "The old name for the top pair is *Orati*, but normally they are simply called wings. They are almost translucent and are the ones humans associate with us. They are also the easiest for humans to see as the other pairs are pure magic and—"

"Wait, other pairs? Plural? I only see one new pair."

Cabel flushed and pulled back. He straightened his shoulder and lifted his head. "Will you always interrupt me when I attempt to share knowledge?"

"It's hard to pull off the haughty look nude, but I like that you try, Princeling." Farren laughed freely as he continued to grip Cabel tightly.

He tried to maintain the expression, but it took only a few seconds for Cabel to laugh too. "You're absurd."

Farren kissed him until Cabel clung to his shoulders then pulled back slowly. "I like it when you smile."

It was difficult not to do so when his happiness made his human happy. It was a thoroughly unique situation despite Cabel's long existence. He accepted another kiss with a grin. His lover then took a deep breath.

"You don't have to tell me about the other wings. I get that I'm not magical and if you—"

Pulling Farren to him, Cabel shut him up with a kiss. The new strategy was one he'd learned from the man under him. "I love that you aren't like me or anyone else I've ever known."

Pink heated Farren's face which also delighted Cabel. His guide had started off cocky and sarcastic, but he'd also found him to be caring and sweet. Too sweet for Cabel to resist more kisses. Without thought, his magic burst through to reveal the final pair of wings. Jerking back, Cabel witnessed the moment Farren noticed the change. It was impossible to miss his expression of awe.

"You are incredible," Farren breathed the words with his gaze locked on the third pair of wings. "What are these called?"

Cabel needed to share the truth, but he also needed a moment. "As I said, the top pair are technically *Orati* though we normally say wings. The largest set is for battle and flight. The technical name is *Petios* though we normally battle wings."

"And this third pair?" Farren still had not looked away from the brightly colored wings.

"*Dorap* is the formal name." Cabel needed to take a breath to continue. "They are also called Mating Wings."

Wide green eyes now studied Farren's face. He found he couldn't look away, but he couldn't speak either.

"Mating...as in *mating*?"

"What do you see?" Cabel ignored the question as his heart raced. He had never shown his mating wings to another. There were legends that a Faeri's lover might see the wings differently than the Faeri himself. Cabel knew his were brightly colored which stood out against the black and red showing his royal lineage. They were also strangely colored compared to paintings in *Agoen*.

Farren stood but kept his hands on Cabel's hips. His gaze locked on the Orati before tracing his secondary pair. Licking his lips, Farren lingered on the glimpse of color now revealed by Cabel's mating wings. He kept one hand on Cabel's hips and moved to stand behind him. Cabel's wings shivered but adjusted to his human's movements.

"It's like a night becoming a new day. The wings at the top look like the moon. Your family colors are the night sky complete with meteor showers and then...these beauties lighten into a sunrise. There are pinks, oranges, and blues. You're gorgeous."

Cabel knew his wings billowed up at the breathy comments, but he tried to remain stoic. "I thought you weren't a morning person."

"I'm not. If you want to wake me up with coffee every morning, I could be." Farren completed his inspection with gentle touches against every wing. His battle pair even pulled aside to reveal more of his mating wings.

It was difficult to wait until Farren stood before him once again before Cabel blurted out the words, "I promise to do just that, *Imisi*."

END OF FLASHBACK

Chapter 16

The memories brought Cabel both pain and pleasure. He'd had a brief, happy moment with Farren. Then Cabel had broken his promise when they'd faced the Dragon the next day. It hadn't been intentional, but he had chosen to protect Farren above everything else. He had ignored his royal duty to the Faeri Court to protect his lover.

"Are you going to explain all of this?"

Turning at the question, Cabel grabbed Farren's arm and pulled him along. It would have been easy to conceal their words, but such actions would also arouse suspicion and shatter any trust he'd built with the Dragon. "I will explain more, but for now, do not worry. The cleansing will prove more powerful with my participation which means your family will be better protected."

"And you? Will you be protected?"

Heart thudding at the question, Cabel nodded. He wanted to touch, kiss, even just stare, but there was no time for such intimacy with the creature monitoring their every move. "I will be fine, *Imisi*."

"If we aren't going to kill each other, I'd like to get one with my day and get my lair back." Phyllia didn't approach but her voice carried easily.

"Yours would've been the only death," Farren retorted before stomping across the cavern.

Phyllia's laughter had Cabel moving quickly to join them. His wings shivered in anticipation of the reveal. The Dragon's amused snort released a plume of smoke. Both he and Farren glared at her.

"Whip those bad boys out, Cabel!"

Gently guiding Farren further away, Cabel rolled his shoulders back. There was no need for the motion, but it eased the tension slightly. He took a deep breath and brought his second set of wings into view. There was no sound from his love at the reveal. Unable to wait, Cabel turned to Farren. His human stood with fisted hands and his attention locked on Cabel's wings. With pure magic filtered through the appendages, they were not only personal and unique but also somewhat independent. His wings fluttered under that intense attention. Of their own accord, they arched up in a showy display causing Phyllia to laugh outright. He snapped them in place behind his back and faced the Dragon.

"I don't suppose you want me to claw those pretty babies, do you?" She lifted a hand to reveal extended shiny, black claws.

"No," Cabel gritted out the answer. He could handle it himself, but it would leave his wings in a weakened condition. If the dust was brushed from the interior portion, flying between the realms or even within the human one wouldn't be an issue.

Farren moved between them giving his back to the Dragon. "If you tell me what to do, I can help."

The only honorable answer was no. Farren did not know his memories had returned. His former lover had chosen not to be close to him previously. "Thank you."

It helped that Phyllia continued to watch them though she did allow them a semblance of privacy by remaining on the other side of the chamber. Cabel sat on a wooden chest with Farren kneeling behind him. His wings pressed eagerly into his love's gentle hands.

Locking his hands together, Cabel took a deep breath and started to explain. "When soft, magic can be collected with simple strokes. If you would, start at the top and go to the tips. Use slow, steady strokes to collect the magic. Once you're finished, clap your hands together to dispel the magic into dust."

Cabel closed his eyes and tried to ignore the feeling of his love's hands gently caressing his wings. The impatient tap of a claw gave him a much-needed distraction and he opened his eyes to glare at the Dragon. The idea of her witnessing their intimacy had Cabel's lips pulling back in a snarl.

"Are you okay? Did I do something wrong?" Farren remained at Cabel's back to ask the questions. His hands were no longer stroking.

Again rolling his shoulders, Cabel shook his head. "No, you are fine. Please continue but do be quick about it."

It was for his own sanity that the delightful torture had to end. The temptation to try his lover's request for a mid-air lovemaking session was too tantalizing. Cabel continued to wrestle his own thoughts as Farren's hands moved more quickly, but still so reverently along his wings. As much as he needed to face some hard truths, Cabel found his mind and body focused on the human touching him so gently.

Farren moved abruptly and even stirred up Cabel's wings with a deliberate touch. "Maybe you could explain the fairy stones to me?"

The sudden movement and question almost had Cabel standing to face his human. He sent magic to straighten his wings and realized his mating wings were visible. Karsia again amplified his power and made all of his wings invisible in the human realm.

"This should be enough, right?" Farren clapped his hands together and sent a shower of sparkles into the container Phyllia provided.

The Dragon was quick to join them and smiled. "Yeah, that will be helpful and worth a great deal more than a few stones."

It wasn't a thank you nor did Cabel expect one. Gratitude came with obligations. "Then we can perform the cleansing ritual now?"

"I have a cave lower—"

Cabel immediately cut the Dragon off, "No, we need a neutral space and I'd prefer to go up, not down."

"Fairies are so picky." Phyllia still led them to another opening with visible stone stairs going up. "I fly from the top. There's a flat space that will be large enough for our circle."

The pale blue sky greeted them once they emerged on the mountaintop. Quartz glistened within the stones and partially explained why the Dragon had selected her lair. The fact that his human kept a careful eye on the creature allowed Cabel to breathe deeply. He reviewed the ritual as he studied the space. Either of them could perform the ritual alone, but their combined power would be greater than the sum of their parts.

Glancing up, Cabel noted the dark clouds hovering on the horizon carried no immediate threat nor did they conceal the blistering sun. Even the Dragon appeared uncomfortable in the still-rising heat and humidity. It was the first time he'd experienced Karsia outside of the Dragon's lair with his memories returned. The abundance of glowing auras below made the presence of magic even more obvious. There was nothing the corruption hadn't touched. His gaze sought Farren's and the existence of the man disputed that thought. His human's golden aura was still soft, welcoming, and beautiful. Magic had not corrupted Farren. Cabel's heart seemingly skipped a beat as he stared at the man he loved.

"If you're through gawking at your bodyguard, we could finish this and move on with our lives." Phyllia stood at the far side of the clearing with her arms crossed over her chest.

"Son of a banshee, couldn't we have worked with a Gnome or even a Troll instead of a Dragon," Farren grumbled just loud enough for Phyllia to hear him.

The Dragon drew her human form up tall and glared. "Keep talking and I may rethink protecting your kind."

Cabel rolled his eyes and stepped between the bickering pair. "Phyllia, if you'll draw the circle, I'll add the elemental points. Farren, you'll need to watch the tunnel and sky while we work."

Phyllia issued a smoky laugh, and his human switched his glare from her to Cabel.

"In other words, stay out of your way?"

There was no chance to argue about how precious his love was as Farren kept talking.

"Fine, I'll play guard, but be careful and don't trust that little snake."

Again, Phyllia could hear the words. The Dragon lifted her chin before flicking out her tongue with a hiss. Cabel stopped Farren with a hand on his arm and leaned forward. Farren's eyes widened before his pupils dilated and he edged even closer.

"Please be careful. As Phyllia isn't the danger, something else lurks in Karsia. You need to stay alert and do not worry about the ritual." Cabel wanted to press a kiss on his lover's mouth, but Farren eased back with a frown.

After scanning the space, his lover ran a hand through his hair and sighed. "You saw something important on the fairy stones, didn't you? Do you know..." His attention shifted to Phyllia and Farren shook his head without finishing the question. "Just be careful."

"I will, *Imisi*." The endearment slipped out and Cabel turned away before Farren could react. Remembering their past when they had no future was a blessing and a curse. It was exactly what Cabel deserved.

"Let's go, Fairy Prince." Phyllia stood just inside a circle watching him.

Gathering the *Agoen* elemental tokens, Cabel stopped at the far edge of the magical boundary. He pulled his energy up to flow through every line in his uniform. Two pairs of wings shuddered into view, leaving only his mating wings hidden. His battle wings were no longer soft but instead sharp and hard. The holly berries heated in his pocket, but Cabel did not pull out his wand. Instead, he stepped over the line and moved counterclockwise to carefully walk the drawn ring.

Magic gathered inside the circle until it rested heavy in the air. The air popped and sizzled when Cabel stopped at the northernmost point. Clouds raced across the sky to hide the sun from their view.

"I need to shift for us to have the most power."

She didn't give him time to disagree before horns extended from her head. The dress shimmered as some of the fabric became scales once more. Her face contorted to reveal more reptilian features with sharpened teeth and oval pupils. In *Agoen*, they would have been able to communicate, but there were more limitations in the human realm. Smoke curled up from slanted nostrils that had sunken into her face.

Phyllia moved to the center of the circle while Cabel flared his wings and allowed them to flap several times. His magic rose fast within him, but his uniform hid any visible signs of power. He couldn't help but look back to see Farren standing guard in the doorway.

Another memory popped up to distract him as he heard his human answer a question he'd ignored only recently.

'This is where I live. The town is named Second Chance. Rumor has it that even magical beings need a second chance sometimes and this is it.'

Chapter 17

This was Cabel's second chance and he had to complete his new mission.

The colors of his Faeri vision brightened as the sounds of Karsia roared loudly in his ears. His magic flared wildly until he heard Farren call his name. Turning, he saw his love watching with wide eyes. Cabel's heart skipped a beat before syncing in Farren's thundering pulse. He took a breath and watched Farren mimic the motion. The riotous magic settled once more as he focused on Farren's golden aura.

Using the blade Farren had returned, Cabel sliced through each token. He sent half fluttering through the air to the Dragon. With a pulse of magic, he sent the *reweial* back to Farren. His human started before wrapping his fingers around the hilt and nodding. As Cabel watched, a line of yellow blossoms began at his human's feet and bloomed quickly to encircle the entire space. A soft breeze cooled the air quickly. The quartz quivered under them as the flowering vine crested over the edges. The Dragon's huff sent sparks and smoke into the air, but Cabel only grinned at Farren.

As he called forth his magic and focused on the elemental tokens, Cabel's thoughts included memories of Farren. He didn't try to push them aside but instead relished the love inside each one. His magic again flared but his uniform embraced the rush of power by chilling him further.

The Dragon shuddered before swaying inside a rising plume of reddish smoke.

Cabel released his magic and stepped forward to walk the perimeter of their circle. He stopped at each cardinal point to place a token.

East – Phoenix feather.

South – Gnome stone.

West – Dragon Scales.

Returning to the North, Cabel completed his chant as he released his personal offering. The sparkling dust covered the ground while also rising to duel with the Dragon's smoke. After only a moment, they exploded together leaving the circle calm and clear.

He clapped his hands and withdrew the holly berries from his pocket. Phyllia did not shift from her Dragon form, but she did turn to watch him. Wand in hand, he sliced cuts at each cardinal point simultaneously. A rush of cooling air greeted them. Cabel directed his attention to Farren and exited at the southern point to join him.

A series of sizzling pops signaled Phyllia's shift and the final steps to destroy their circle and complete the ritual.

STEPPING FROM THE DRAGON'S cabin and back into Karsia brought them all to a sudden halt. Farren continued off the porch to trail his fingers along the holly bushes lining the trail.

"It's gotta be twenty degrees cooler out here." The sunlight only made Farren's aura brighten. He trailed a finger over the dark, spiky leaves before tapping a cluster of red berries. "I guess we needed a Faeri to make the cleansing ritual work."

Phyllia's laugh was more of an annoyed huff and included a circle of smoke. She strolled toward Farren while giving the holly bushes a wide berth. "It's still just a pebble in the pond, little human. Karsia will need more work just to keep the corruption from spreading. We haven't found a way to reverse the magic."

Taking a deep breath to enjoy the cooler air, Cabel stepped off the porch...until an icy shaft lanced through his heart to embed in his head. The air got stuck in his lungs and every muscle in his body locked in a painful cramp. Another rush of new memories filled his mind.

Silver – pain – lies – darkness.

'You chose poorly.'

Fairy stones – chess pieces – storms.

Dishonor.

"Hey, sweetheart. Look at me. Are you okay?"

Farren suddenly appeared to dominate Cabel's view of the world. Distantly, he heard Phyllia speaking, but he couldn't understand her. For Farren, he managed to nod once as a familiar pain hammered his mind.

Blood – suspicion.

A choice.

A mistake.

Death.

Fire chased the memories away, but the truth remained. Cabel gasped and blinked repeatedly. He was now sitting on the porch cradled in Farren's arms. His lover's heart thudded fast and hard.

"Breathe with me." Farren released his death grip on Cabel to stroke a hand up and down his back. "That's it. Deep breaths."

"Drink this." Phyllia offered a mug with a cartoon-like fairy on it. She shrugged and then smiled gently. "Humans say laughter is the best medicine."

The welcoming scent of honey and jasmine teased Cabel. When he reached for the mug, Farren grabbed it and held it to his lips. The warm refreshment further eased the pain.

"Don't glare at me. I'm hardly going to poison him considering what we've done together." The Dragon quickly lifted both hands and shook her head. "I'm not grateful or indebted for the ritual. That's simply what happened."

"It's fine. I'm fine." Cabel was reluctant to push away from Farren but he did return the cup to Phyllia. The new memories were too pressing to linger though. "We must leave now."

Farren's mouth fell open until he snapped it shut and frowned. With wide eyes, the Dragon put a little distance between them and her.

"How can we do that when stepping off the porch almost knocked you on your fairy ass? What happened? What's going on?"

With the new dangers still fluttering in his mind, Cabel pushed away and stood on his own. He glanced at the Dragon before smiling at his lover. "It's time to drop a boulder."

"How exactly can we do that?" Phyllia asked.

Farren moved to stand in front of him. "You know something."

If the woman hadn't been with them...if he hadn't lost his memories, Cabel would have revealed his mistakes. "I think we need to return to your town, and I need to talk to my cousin. It'll take a couple of days, right?" He'd get some time alone with Farren before—

"How about just a few minutes instead?" The Dragon shifted partially to reveal large, leathery wings.

"No, absolutely not," Farren denied.

Giggling, Phyllia hid her wings once more. "I discovered a *lanua* to a witch's garden."

"A doorway," Cabel explained without looking away from the Dragon. "Does the witch know you use it? Does anyone else use it?"

"Calm down, your human will be safe. I asked the witch for permission, and she uses it as well. She's just a little thing, old as the hills, I suspect, and her name is—"

"Leina."

Cabel and Phyllia turned to look at Farren. His human only shrugged before gathering his bags once more.

The Dragon held up a hand and returned to her cabin for just a few seconds. She returned with a small red bag. "We had no deal, so this is a barter offering."

She didn't explain what her offering was, but she did nod toward Farren's bag. Cabel started shaking his head before Farren could offer anything.

"It's the way of Karsia, snowfly. There's no disrespect intended, nor any obligation." Phyllia held the bag out and smiled when Farren stepped forward to take it.

He looked down into his own bag then offered a small vial with only a few drops of back inside. Phyllia released a high-pitched squeal and grabbed it. She opened and closed her mouth several times without speaking. Farren chuckled and closed his bag once more.

The Dragon started toward her door when she paused next to Cabel. "Take care of him."

"I will," Farren agreed with a wink.

Phyllia looked from Cabel to Farren. "I think you too deserve each other. Perhaps, we'll meet again, snowfly." With a final wave, she closed the door behind herself.

"You know she was talking to me." Cabel tried for a stern expression but couldn't quite manage not to smile.

"She didn't say your name," Farren refuted. He tossed the offered bag into the air and caught it. "I guess there's some protocol that says we can't open this yet, right?"

Cabel walked by his human when he saw the spark of red lighting up the Dragon's portal. He smiled when he heard the rustling of the fabric. "Yes, of course...so go ahead and do it."

"Are these Dragon scales?" Farren peered into the bag then held it out to Cabel.

Tipping the bag over sent several red and green scales into his palm. "Yes, and from more than one Dragon. These are valuable. What did you give her?"

"Cacao beans. She had several drawers of chocolate, so I figured it was a safe bet."

Nodding, Cabel couldn't stop a laugh. "You just gave a chocolate hoarding Dragon the means to grow her own hoard. Yes, that was a safe bet."

"There were also orange seeds in there. Hopefully, she won't be too disappointed. I'm not sure I'd like to have her as an enemy." Farren accepted the offering back and stuffed it inside his bag.

Cabel stopped at the entrance to the cave.

"Did the portal thing have to be down the dark cave?" Farren stepped forward with an exaggerated sigh.

Blinking at the rush of hot air, Cabel led the way deeper inside. "It's not far."

Farren struck his firestone, and the tunnel was lit by a bright pink light. "Leina was the one who gave this to me. If this thing is hers, then we'll be fine. How does it work though?"

They'd arrived at the bronze gate and Cabel studied the symbols carved into it. "It says it belongs to Leina."

"Can Phyllia read that?" Farren used a single finger to trace the first symbol.

Cabel shook his head. "It's written in *Solegn* which was supposedly the language of angels. Your Leina may be very old indeed if she knew angels. They roamed the human realm millennia ago. It was during the first separation when *Agoen* was locked. I don't even know anyone who has met an angel."

When Farren didn't reply, Cabel pulled his attention away from the old language. His human didn't seem worried or even impatient. Farren appeared to be waiting for Cabel to finish his inspection. "You don't even blink at magical reveals."

"I can't change the world or others. Plus, Leina has been good to me and the town."

His chuckling stopped Farren from explaining further. Cabel squeezed his shoulder and grinned. "If it doesn't kill you..."

Farren rolled his eyes. "Live and let live isn't a bad policy, snowfly. Now, are we going through the gate or not?"

Elbowing his love in the side, Cabel held his hand out. "I need the *reweial* to offer my blood."

"Of course, you do. Why knock when you can bleed?" Rolling his eyes, Farren handed the weapon over. "Why don't you just keep the blade this time?"

It took only a few drops of blood to open the gate. "Stay behind and step on the same stones I step on. This portal leads to other realms, and we need to return to your home."

"Watch you walk and follow. Got it."

He released a loud sigh and grinned when Farren snorted a laugh. It was a nice, new memory and Cabel would treasure it. If his plan didn't work out...

Chapter 18

Stepping carefully, Cabel breathed in the light, fresh scent of flowers. "Your Leina must really like gardens."

"Should my ears be ringing?"

"There's a lot of magic here," Cabel agreed. He brushed a hand against a white bloom that appeared directly in front of him. Plucking it, he handed it back over his shoulder. "Hold this."

There was a moment of silence before Farren spoke again.

"Yeah, that helped...which does make you good in my book." Farren cleared his throat before continuing, "I'm guessing you aren't going to fill me in on your discovery or your plan, are you?"

Cabel wasn't sure how to answer his love. "It's not much further. I'm not sure where on the witch's property we'll end up. Stay close to me."

When he paused to allow the next gate to appear, Farren pressed against his back. The man didn't back away, but he did place a hand on Cabel's hip to steady himself. Farren leaned against him for only a second. Straightening up, he pushed through the gate to see wall-to-wall flowers. Farren peered over his shoulder as there was no space for them to stand together.

The flowers fluttered to create a narrow path for them to follow.

"At least we won't get lost," Farren whispered as he remained close behind.

They emerged from the garden to see the road mere feet away. Cabel felt his magic surge as the witch's power pulled back. The *Omil* crystal appeared before him, and he wrapped his fingers around it. With only a small burst of power, he could see Alida.

"There you are. I was getting worried. Are you okay?"

Farren moved a distance away, but Alida had already seen him.

"Was that your guide?"

He'd only have a few moments to speak as Farren could return quickly. "The Dragon was not the issue. There's something else going on here."

"Have you reported that to Rister? He stopped by and invited me to *Agoen* but—"

"No," Cabel interrupted her much more loudly than he'd intended. Farren glanced up from his phone but didn't return. "Do not trust any Faeri and do not go to *Agoen*. Keep your witches close for protection, Alida. I can't explain yet, but you need to stay in Tellum."

Reid appeared into view and a black and white cat jumped into Alida's arms.

"What's going on? Are you in danger?"

"I can't explain—"

"Try to anyway," Reid spoke over Cabel with a glare. "You can't just pop in out and out and scare her like this."

The cat meowed loudly as if to agree with the witch. Cabel glanced at Farren who was now speaking into his phone. "We worked with the Dragon to cleanse the lands, but the magic has been corrupted to an incredible degree and it wasn't the Dragon."

"Who did it?"

Cabel wasn't ready to voice his thoughts, so he shook his head. "We are in the town of Second Chance in Karsia. If you don't hear from me in a few days, reach out to Zaniel and—"

"No, come back here now and we'll all go back together to face whatever it is. If you tell me honor requires you to face it alone, Cabel, I'll kill you myself." Alida only closed her mouth when Reid hugged her close.

"I am sorry. You are safer there, but the people here will need help if I fail again. Ask Zaniel for guidance and don't be afraid to work with the Dragons. Keep working on your Jacek and Tanwen research too. It might prove useful."

Alida lifted her head from Reid's shoulder to peer at him. "Useful would be you telling me what's going on and not endangering your life again. I don't actually like our extended family so you're it for me. Flappy fairy wings!"

A girlish giggle had Cabel turning to the side where Farren held Zoe in his arms. Lilly stood next to them wearing a big smile. It was Zoe who captured his attention and the small child managed to smirk at him. He hid the *reweial* without looking away from the child.

"Someone is in trouble," Lilly almost sang the words.

"Who is that?" Alida moved closer to the crystal as if she could turn the crystal herself to see the others.

"Lilly came to greet us, and she shared that another fairy is currently in town." Farren smiled at the little girl, but his expression was much grimmer when he met Cabel's gaze. "His name is Rister."

"Didn't you just tell me to avoid—"

"Alida!" Cabel was forced to raise his voice as he couldn't stop his cousin otherwise. "Check with Zaniel in a few days and you can meet Lilly in person. I know you'll adore her."

His cousin got the message and gritted her teeth. "I'm holding you to that."

"I do love you. You know that, right?" Cabel had to look away from Zoe to focus on Alida.

She sniffed and gave him a series of small nods. "I do. You should also know I tolerate you. Please be careful, Cabel."

"I will." Cabel clicked off the crystal by withdrawing his magic. It was difficult not to stare at Zoe while he mentally updated the specifics of his plan. "Lilly, could you please ask your mom to get everyone inside until Farren returns."

It wasn't a question and Lilly spun immediately on her heel until Farren placed a hand on her shoulder.

"Take Zoe with you, Lady Lilly. I'll be there shortly." Farren leaned down to kiss her cheek before trying to shift the baby into the girl's arms. Zoe clung to his neck despite his best efforts.

"She won't go, and she shouldn't. You need her." Cabel stepped forward to steer Lilly to face town once more. "Go now, Lilly, and don't stop until you're inside your house with your mom."

Farren moved Zoe to a more comfortable position and glared at Cabel. "Care to fill in the blanks for me?"

"There's no time. I wish there was...but I need to leave with Rister. It's the only way to protect your people. He won't pay any attention to you. Zoe, you need to hide yourself." Cabel saw the baby nod.

Farren leaned away from her to look from one to the other. "If this Rister guy is dangerous, you shouldn't leave with him. You're safer here."

"But you won't be, and neither will the ones you love." Cabel took a moment to feel the magic in Second Chance. It was different and his mentor was responsible. "I can't fail again."

"Then let me help you," Farren argued.

Cabel watched Rister turn the corner and stop to stare at them. The powerful Faeri's silver uniform was nearly blinding. Inclining his head, Cabel started forward with measured steps. There would be only a few seconds to explain to Farren before his mentor would be able to hear them. "Please listen carefully. Zoe is a Phoenix who bonded to you. She is locked into her form's natural life until she comes of age. This means she may understand much, but she won't be able to help you. Her magic will provide formidable protection though."

"She's a...you can see that?" Farren stared at the child who met and held his gaze. A golden feather fluttered into existence between them. "Okay, she's a Phoenix. Got it. We'll deal with that later. Right now, I'm more worried about you."

There would be further explanations and Cabel would have no chance to declare his love. Rister was close enough to overhear their words. Any efforts to stop him would let the Faeri know the truth.

Shaking his head, Cabel placed a hand on Farren's shoulder. "Go play with Lilly. She's expecting you."

Farren gritted his teeth and glared at Rister. "You know my town's name."

With his thoughts on his mentor, the words meant nothing to Cabel. He was still trying to ensure his memories were clear and accurate. Mistaking the truth could be deadly.

"You can use your magic easily now," Farren continued.

The hidden meaning of the comments suddenly became too clear. Cabel stumbled to a stop and faced his lover. There was no chance to defend his choices.

"That's what I thought." Farren nodded to himself and again stared at Rister. "It doesn't matter what you know. It matters what I know, and I know I have to protect those I love."

Rister joined them with his wings almost perfectly still behind him. "Isn't that sweet? I believe I've warned you in the past that human lovers are very clingy, Cabel. Send the boy on his way so we can talk. I wish to hear about your mission."

Cabel was weighing his options when Farren stepped in front of him.

"We didn't kill the Dragon. Actually, we worked with her."

With a burst of blue light, metallic grey wings hardened into view behind Rister. He ignored the humans to stare at Cabel. "That is unfortunate. I had such high hopes for you."

Chapter 19

Cabel felt the rush of magic recede and studied the new landscape around them. A crystal-clear lake glistened at the edge of the barren space. The only plant life was a ring of mushrooms encircling them. Not only had Rister transported Farren and Zoe, but there were also three unknown humans standing a short distance away. He pulled Farren's arm and tried to stand between the pair and any threat.

"You need not worry about the Orions, Cabel. They are only here to take the baby Phoenix where it belongs."

"You're the reason supernaturals here are hunted and killed? Why help humans kill your own kind. I thought Fairies were about honor."

Appreciating Farren's bravery and wanting to keep his human alive were two very different things. Cabel tightened his grip on the man's wrist when Rister turned slowly to stare at him.

"The beasts have stolen magic that doesn't belong to them. I'm merely collecting what's rightfully Faeri." Rister's wings twitched then stilled once more. "Of course, humans have nothing of interest for me. Had you stayed quiet, you might have lived."

Both Farren and Zoe tightened their embrace as two Orions approached. Cabel had only one option. He drew his *reweial* and struck one of Rister's battle wings. The almost metallic edge to the collision had the Hunters freezing in place. Farren cuddled Zoe close and tried to protect her.

Cabel stood still after making the challenge; Rister's eyes flashed silver as he unsheathed his sword.

"I accept your challenge, Cabel Orlaith. You will wish I had killed you with mercy. Honor demands a high price." His mentor grinned suddenly and then laughed. "How perfect. I told you love weakened a Faeri and now you'll die to prove those words."

He heard Farren moving but Rister's smugness demanded Cabel's attention. A Faeri duel offered both a chance and love wouldn't weaken him. Fear pierced his heart as he wondered if he'd missed some other truth that could hurt Farren and Zoe.

"As you know, we are only allowed our own weapons, no wands," Rister intoned seriously before he sliced his sword through the air. The myriad of jewels created a rainbow of sparkles. "That *reweial* does not belong to you."

The deep vibrations in the blade carried a warmth Cabel now recognized. Belief didn't change truth, but at least Farren would be able to protect himself if Cabel failed again. He bowed his head slightly and offered the weapon to his lover hilt first.

"What? No. That's yours, not mine. I don't want it." The last words carried a frantic edge and his human wrapped both arms around Zoe without reaching for the *reweial*.

Rister's laughter was overly loud. "It matters not what you want, human. When Cabel gave you his weapon, the magic in the blade accepted his wishes. That *reweial* has been weakened by the bond. You would have lacked the power to kill even the rogue Dragon."

Cabel accepted the odds of his survival had diminished but he nodded. "All will be as it is meant to be. Let the human leave—"

"No," Farren interrupted. He shifted Zoe to the side and drew his own weapon. "If he can give me his blade, I can give him this one. Take it."

Smiling, Cabel started to deny the gift, but Rister spoke first.

"I accept the offering. Cabel may use the blade if that is what you wish."

"It is," Farren agreed immediately.

"Then Cabel will fight for the both of you and, when he loses, you too shall forfeit your life," Rister announced.

"No."

"Yes."

Sending a quick frown at Farren for disagreeing with him, Cabel then focused on Risten/ Rister once more. "You cannot bind a human to a Faeri duel. I have not accepted the weapon."

"*Agoen* law honors human free will. Do you dispute that?"

This time, Cabel ignored Rister and strode to face Farren. "Zoe needs you. Alida needs you. You cannot bind your fate to mine."

"There's a simple answer here, Princeling." Farren winked and again offered his weapon. "Don't lose."

Memories of his lover's cocky smile flashed brightly in Cabel's mind. His body warmed even as his thoughts conjured images of Farren winking at him in the future as they shared a coffee at sunrise. Unconcerned about their audience, Cabel crashed his mouth into Farren's for a hard kiss. He pulled back and held the human weapon in his hand. "Thank you, *Imisi*."

The duel wasn't an abstract manner of honor. Cabel had to fight so Farren could live. He faced Rister with a swagger he'd learned from his other half.

His mentor's nose wrinkled before he lifted his chin. "You could have been great, Cabel. I gave you so many chances. It will almost be a shame to end your life now."

"Your actions have brought shame on your family line, Rister, and on all Fairies. You're the one corrupting Karsia by murdering humans and twisting magic. I am honored to fight for Farren of Karsia." Even as he spoke the words, accepting the truth settled the ache in Cabel's chest. He turned once more and smiled at his lover. The kiss he offered was soft and gentle this time. "My heart remembered before my mind did, but it doesn't change the truth. I love you."

Farren's eyes widened, and he started to shake his head before he huffed a laugh. "Of course you'd say that now. If you finish off that piece of trash, we can go home and make new memories."

"Take the Phoenix," Rister ordered with a snarl.

"No." Cabel and Farren spoke the dental together with Zoe frowning at Rister.

The Orions moved forward to follow the order. Farren reached for his weapon but merely plucked a smaller blade Cabel hadn't seen before from the hilt. His human threw it with deadly accuracy to pierce one Hunter's jugular. The two others hesitated and looked to Rister. Cabel didn't give his mentor a chance to direct them. He drew his wand and released a chilling blast. The Orions were knocked back into the lake which immediately iced over.

Rister made no effort to rescue them. He only watched with a slight frown. "If you can kill humans so easily, there may still be hope for you. Why not stand with me as ruler over this realm?"

"Humans have a right to their realm. Magic may find any being worthy and that is not for you to decide." Cabel swung the heavier weapon through the air. "It is not your honor that I defend now but my own. I do not intend to lose."

Years of training with Rister prepared Cabel for the rapid-fire swipes, feints, and lunges. Without his *reweial* to absorb the magic, his arms soon trembled with the effort to block Rister's blows. Cabel did manage to use his wings for his own strikes. His slower movements allowed Rister's wings to pierce his body too many times.

Silver tipped in blood red.

Icy chills and puffing breaths.

Pain.

Stumbling back, Cabel heard Farren curse. He still barely stopped the blade from touching the ground. The air around them chilled with the bloody battle and magic hummed in the air.

"I gave you a second chance already. I won't do so again." Rister's *reweial* glistened with silver sparkles and Cabel's blood.

Cabel noted the green tinge to his blade and lifted it slightly. "It wasn't a second chance for me when you stole my memories. You were only trying to keep a loyal warrior blind to do your dishonor."

Rister's wings trembled at the insult and then he lunged forward.

Blades clashed and clanged as the tinny scent of blood coated the air. Wings swiped, colder and harder than their blades. Cabel faltered under the barrage of blows and landed hard on one knee.

"You can die as the humans you killed." Instead of using his *reweial* or his wings, Rister drew out a long, glowing red wand and flicked it to the side. The lake shuddered before the ice Cabel had created floated through the air toward them.

"No," Farren cried out before cutting off further words.

The ice surged closer allowing Rister's magic to carve it into sharpened points.

"Your choice changed nothing, Cabel. Not only will your human die, but the sleeping lovers will never awaken. We will drive the Dragons underground and I will rule this land and *Agoen*." Rister's eyes glowed silver as his voice rose in pitch. He slashed his wand through the air.

Cabel lifted his head and waited for the killing strike. Warm raindrops splattered lightly on his face. Farren's chuckling and Zoe's cooing was the only sound in the stillness.

"If wands aren't allowed, doesn't that mean he cheated?"

Rister sputtered before glaring at Cabel. "Does your human pet not know this is beyond him? His paltry weapon won't even pierce my flesh."

Squeezing the hilt with his pinky, Cabel felt for the hidden latch. A smaller blade emerged, and he grabbed the handle. It took only a second to aim and send the dagger flying through the air. It landed true and impaled Rister's throat. Not a killing blow for a Faerie, but his smirk wavered before he could remove the weapon. His flesh darkened immediately as the Dragon scales coating the blade poisoned his blood.

He landed with a thud. The white light was warm and nearly blinding. When Cabel opened his eyes, only a pile of fairy stones remained. He needed no time to mourn as Farren slid to a stop next to him in the dirt with Zoe still in his arms.

"That was surprisingly tame for a supernatural battle. I thought there'd be fireworks or at least glitter." Though Farren teased, his face was pale, and his eyes ran over Cabel's body repeatedly. "How injured are you? What can I do?"

"I'm sorry," Cabel began before coughing.

"What? What the fox do you mean? You're gonna be fine." Hands trembling, Farren moved Zoe to one side and his free hand hovered in the air over Cabel's chest.

Cabel grabbed Farren's hand and smiled. "I will be fine. I'm sorry my choices hurt you and that I didn't tell you I had my memories back. I thought..."

"You thought you were doing the right thing. Yeah, I've heard that one before." Farren shook his head but still smiled. He also removed several bottles from his pack and handed them over. "These were the last of Leina's gifts when she told me that even magic needed a second chance to make the right choice."

Chapter 20

After drinking the healing potions, Cabel's mind was clear of the overwhelming pain. His body was still tired as was his magic. He couldn't even call forth his wings. As his mind was clear, he managed to frown at Farren. "What do you mean Leina told you?"

Farren kept Zoe close as she released a hiccupping cry. "Is she okay? I didn't think she could access her magic in this form."

Even weak, he could see the baby Phoenix in her true form. "She's tired too and needs to sleep, but she'll be okay." He managed to conjure soft blankets and a fluffy pillow for the child. Most Phoenix maintained a bird-like appreciation for nests and Zoe did close her eyes and smile.

His human settled the child without meeting his gaze, but Cabel had no intention of letting either of them escape. "We need to talk about this. Would you prefer to speak first, or should I?"

Still focused on the Phoenix, Farren didn't immediately reply. Cabel released another wave of magic to make the space more hospitable for them as well and leaned against the pillow now at his back. He smiled when he noticed the color choice was overwhelming gold to match his lover's aura. It wasn't a conscious choice, but it wasn't a surprising one either. "I fell in love with you twice. I know we 'switch' sexually, but would you prefer I lead this conversation?"

Half groaning, half laughing, Farren finally looked up. "I'll never understand how you can be formal and blunt at the same time." He scrubbed a hand over his face and then through his hair.

"I assumed the Tellum doctors were right, and that the Dragon's magic had cost me my memories. Some things came to me in pieces while resting, but I found them difficult to understand or accept." Cabel paused when Farren nodded.

"Faeries don't dream."

"Precisely," Cabel confirmed. He accepted a bottle of water as his lover sought a physical distraction and rummaged through his bag. "When you gave me the *reweial* back, time froze and most of my memories returned. I'm sorry I forgot you and our love, even for a second. I know my second chance hurt you."

Farren's jaw tightened, and he looked away to swallow then licked his lips.

"I thought you were just moody and flighty like most humans." Cabel relished his love's burst of laughter at his teasing. However, he didn't reach for the man as he wanted to do. "I promised never to hurt you, and I broke that vow."

Already shaking his head, Farren stopped laughing. "No, you didn't. I know how Faeri promises work, but real life, real love isn't that black and white. I know you were trying to do what was best. You were suspicious of Rister when we visited *Agoen*. I can see that now."

"I was, but I still believed he'd act with honor. I didn't understand the depth of his betrayal until I saw him after we fought the Dragon the first time. It wasn't Phyllia's magic that robbed me of my memories. It was Rister giving me a second chance." The words tasted bitter on Cabel's tongue and his lips curled back.

"You coated the small blade in Dragon scales as soon as we returned to Karsia. Maybe you should have used them on the big blade and saved yourself some pain." Farren leaned forward to brush a hand over Cabel's face and he couldn't resist leaning into the touch. "Are you sure you're okay?"

Cabel smiled even as he missed Farren's touch. "I will be and using that much magic on a human weapon would have ruined the surprise. Rister underestimated it and you."

"So did you, Princeling."

There was no denying the truth of those teasing words. "I did. It didn't take me as long this time to realize how incredible you are."

As usual, Farren flushed at the praise. Cabel hoped for more opportunities to again kiss such words of love and adoration into his lover's heated flesh. He pulled his gaze back to Farren's face and found the man watching him carefully with bright green eyes. Moving slowly, Cabel cupped his face and paused. Farren nodded once and leaned forward.

Their lips met in a familiar and welcome warmth. Soft and gentle, the kiss was a new exploration and a physical promise. His body certainly remembered his lover and responded enthusiastically. Cabel had always preferred the chill of *Agoen*...until he'd met Farren. It hadn't been the human's lands his heart ached for, but the human himself. "I need you."

"Right back ya," Farren moaned his agreement.

His lover pushed and pulled to get him flat on his back and Cabel didn't fight the efforts. He did everything possible to pull Farren even closer to him.

Jerking back upright, Farren scrubbed a hand over his face. He paused and pressed his fingers against his kiss-swollen lips. "Son of a banshee."

Freezing in place, Cabel couldn't even breathe while waiting to see what was wrong. Farren cupped his face and kissed him with a grin before shaking his head.

"I don't know much about kids, but I can't imagine Zoe should see what I want you to do to me and what I want to do to you."

It took hearing the man's laugh for Cabel to understand the words instead of the memories and dreams playing in his mind. "I can fix that."

Farren swallowed hard but didn't look away from him. "Then fix it."

He took a second to breathe and focus. His magic rose with surprising ease considering the recent battle. The soft pink bubble made Farren chuckle and even Zoe woke to blink at the sparkling lights. She immediately snuggled back into her impromptu nest and closed her eyes.

"We can see and hear her, but she can't see or hear us. Now, If I do remember correctly, we—"

"Not funny, Princeling," Farren interrupted the amnesia reference. He shook his head but pulled Cabel back into his arms and under him.

Nuzzling against his lover's neck, Cabel pressed several kisses there before pulling back. "I still owe you a mid-air orgasm."

"You do, but you also just fought your mentor, and I don't want to land on my bare ass in the dirt. We're gonna hold off on the magical lovemaking. I don't think I want to wait for prep though. It's been torture being close to you without being *close* to you." Farren may have started with a teasing tone, but his voice cracked at the end.

Cabel reassured Farren with another gentle kiss. His love blushed at verbal praise and melted into soft touches. The man deserved both and more. Cabel deepened the kiss to resist the temptation to make more promises that could break his lover's heart.

Teasing nips and playful licks became more urgent.

Hands clutched instead of caressed.

Comforting warmth became a sizzling heat.

"Fox this. Can you just?" Farren's hips jerked, and he almost whimpered without completing the request.

There was no turning back at Farren's words. Cabel pushed up and flipped them, so his human was lying beneath him. A mere thought removed their clothes in a chilling rush that did nothing to dampen his ardor. Cabel wanted everything at once – tenderness and heat, loving promises. He simply wanted Farren.

"We'll do the magical lovemaking later too. I've waited too long." Farren flipped them over and ground their cocks together with a roll of his hips. "There's nothing wrong with fast and dirty. That's how humans like it sometimes."

The attempt to tease wasn't less effective for Farren's gasping as they rutted together. Cabel was lost in the pleasure of the skin-on-skin contact until he looked up. Heavy-lidded, his lover's green eyes were dominated by dilated pupils. The need to please his lover was the most important thing in any realm.

"I do love a human so fast and dirty works for me."

Hips stuttering, Farren crashed their mouths together for several seconds. He back bowed ending their kiss. "Can't wait, don't wanna wait."

Cabel brushed his mouth over the extended column of Farren's throat when the man allowed his head to fall back. "Then you do not need to wait, *Imisi*."

Seeing the man's body tense and hearing the sounds of his pleasure, heat flowed through Cabel and pooled low in his body. There was no way he could wait either considering Farren's need. He tugged Farren to rest on one elbow and wrapped their hands around both of their shafts. Another burst of magic provided a tingling wetness.

"I love the magical lube," Farren ground out. "Together. I want you to come with me."

"Together," Cabel managed to grit out the promise before Farren dropped his head to rest their foreheads together.

Gasping breaths.

White-hot pressure.

Shared pleasure.

Cabel felt their hearts racing together even before Farren collapsed against him. He did manage to clean them up even as he wrapped his arms around his lover. Smiling, Cabel embraced the happiness filling him—

An overwhelming press of magic pulled them apart.

Chapter 21

When the magic disappeared, Cabel blinked and saw his cousin. He moved in front of Farren as Alida started to cover her eyes. "Whoa, is that a kid?"

"That's your question?" Cabel switched his glare from his cousin to the witches and then finally to Zaniel when the being laughed. "Why did you bring us here?"

"I foolishly thought you were in trouble. Nothing in our last conservation said you were getting busy with your guide. You spoke of danger and betrayal. I won't rush to save your winged ass next time." Alida's wings fluttered as she knelt next to the glowing pink orb.

Farren choked on a laugh as Cabel felt a rush of guilt.

"Be glad I distracted her so you could finish and find your—"

"La la la," Alida interrupted loudly. She continued to focus on Zoe. "You could magic some clothes or something. I don't need to see or hear about the dirty bits. Who is this adorable kid?"

Cabel did provide fresh clothes to his human and allowed his uniform to cover himself. He turned to check on Farren as Alida screamed. Pivoting around, he saw the pink ball was now flaming orange. The fire disappeared with a pop and Zoe sat on the floor glaring at the strangers. Her fierce expression melted into a sweet smile when Farren brushed by Cabel to pick her up.

"So, she's..." Alida was now positioned between the Debare brothers. All three stared at the scene.

"A Phoenix," Cabel confirmed. He met Farren in the middle of the room and embraced Zoe when she reached for him. "Farren rescued her from Orions and she's bonded to him."

"I have a niece? I have a niece." Alida launched herself forward with a delighted laugh. "Hello, little one. I'm going to be your favorite aunt and we'll have so much fun!"

Zoe stared for several seconds before smiling at his cousin. Something inside of Cabel loosened as Alida laughed and Zoe joined in.

"I'm guessing no one is gonna argue with her, right? They'd be cousins, but okay." Reid exchanged a look with his brother who shrugged. "I guess we have a niece then."

"Family can be by choice. Zoe chose Farren who chose Cabel. I can choose to be an aunt if Zoe is okay with that." Alida offered a hand and Zoe took it. His cousin pressed a loud kiss against the baby's hand causing her to giggle. "See? We're family. Right?"

They hadn't quite talked everything out, but it was an easy question for Cabel. "Yes, we are."

"We have a lot to talk about," Farren spoke up. He moved Zoe to the side to stare at Cabel. "You can't just do your thing without telling me anymore. Either we're partners and you trust me—"

"I do and we are," Cabel rushed to reply. He didn't care that the Debare brothers laughed at his eagerness. He only cared that Farren nodded. They'd spoken of bonding previously...before he'd forgotten their love and broken Farren's heart. He had no right to expect to pick up where they'd left off.

"If I'm now responsible for a baby Phoenix, having Faeri backup wouldn't be bad," Farren conceded causing the witches to laugh again. He frowned when he caught Cabel's grimace.

Blowing out a sigh, Cabel glanced at his cousin and the man he loved. "Let's just say fairy going forward. Faeri reminds me too much of Rister. I'm good with being a fairy in the human realm."

"Flapping fairy wings," Alida exclaimed before clapping. "It's about time you see the beauty in humanity."

Cabel leaned close to kiss Farren. "I definitely see the beauty here."

His love rolled his eyes before closing the distance for another kiss.

"I hate to break up the love fest, but does that mean we missed the battle?" Reid redirected the conversation.

There was a lot to discuss, but Cabel only moved closer to Farren and intertwined their fingers. His body warmed when his love smiled at him.

"There wasn't much of a battle as Cabel kicked Rister's as...butt. I guess we shouldn't curse in front of the kid, right?" Farren shook his head and tightened his grip on Cabel's hand.

"I've told you forever that Rister was a bag of troll nuts," Alida almost cooed the words as she continued to focus on Zoe.

"Yes, that is the pertinent part of this discussion." Cabel kept his face blank until his cousin glared and then he winked at her. "Rister has been working with Orions to capture magical beings. He also corrupted the magic in Karsia."

Farren frowned and shook his head. "I still don't get how that helped him. It did draw out the Dragons, but he still sent you to fix the supposed problem."

"The Court also kept the Dragon problem a secret," Lian added.

"What do you think he was doing? He was your mentor. Does it make sense to you?" Reid edged closer when Zoe noted his colorful tattoos.

Cabel met Zaniel's gaze, but he remained quiet. Nodding to himself, Cabel shared his thoughts. "I don't think he meant to corrupt it. He wanted to release it so he could capture it for himself. He wouldn't have been able to steal magic in *Agoen*, but Karsia doesn't have magical laws.

"Blaming the Dragons was just a perk then," Farren concluded.

"He was really making a move to rule both realms?" Alida convinced Zoe to let her hold her and bounced the child happily. "I'm glad you're here and he's not."

The fact that the witches nodded gave Cabel pause. "The problem is that I don't think he was working alone. He also referenced keeping

Jacek and Tanwen sleeping. Without that union guiding *Agoen*, there will still be chaos and danger. And those issues will still bleed out onto humans."

"How do we wake up a pair of legendary lovers?"

Cabel had no answer for Farren, but Alida immediately glared at them.

"If you'd bothered to share what you were doing, I could have helped." Alida crossed her arms over her chest and stared Cabel down for several seconds. "It's about reuniting the elements and bringing peace to magic. Earth grounds Fire but there's still Wind and Rain. There's more to it than that. Right, Zaniel?"

Zaniel was nowhere to be seen.

"Son of a banshee. I knew we shouldn't trust him. We need to get out of here." Cabel withdrew his wand and started seeking to reveal the magic.

"I'm sorry. Did you just use a human curse?" Alida's mouth hung open as she burst into laughter. "Farren, you are my hero."

He couldn't argue with his cousin, especially as Farren blushed so beautifully once again. Instead, Cabel kissed his cheek.

"Maybe we should focus on the problems at hand?" His lover scanned the beautiful garden and then frowned. "Where are we?"

"A back room in Zaniel's store," Lian supplied the answer and grinned as he lifted a hand to point to a glowing exit sign that hung in mid-air. "Nope, we can't explain it either."

Cabel nodded to Zoe and Farren accepted the child back from Alida. He waited until his love stood behind him to move toward the exit. With only a brief press of energy, they emerged into a normal-looking street. He turned back to see everyone was safe and Zaniel's store was behind them. Humans walked the street in the warm sunlight as if everything was normal. Red and green holiday decorations dotted the street. When Farren sucked in a quick breath, Cabel pivoted to face him. His lover winced and dragged his teeth over his lip before meeting Cabel's gaze.

"Everything has changed, but she was right about...well, everything."

Taking Farren's free hand in his once again, Cabel didn't break eye contact. "Everything has changed, but not the fact that I love you. You are everything to me, you and Zoe. If you still want to bond, I'll find a way to protect you both."

Alida gasped and didn't bother respecting their privacy. "Oh, we can have a Christmas bonding ceremony. I've never been to one but—"

The words stopped when Reid placed a hand over her mouth. Alida frowned but remained quiet when the witch removed his hand. Farren was watching their antics with a smile and then he turned back to Cabel with a serious expression.

"I do still want that. Leina gave me all the potions we've used, and she said red and gold must be bound before the Cold Moon. I'm not sure exactly what she meant but your family color is red—"

"And your aura is gold," Cabel completed the thought. He remembered revealing that fact and the night of love that had followed. "I want to bind my life to you, Farren of Karsia."

"Oh, this is beautiful." Alida's whisper was anything but quiet.

Farren pulled him in for a kiss before Cabel could even glare at his cousin. "Yes, let's do the bonding thing."

It took a second for Cabel to realize the heat in his chest was more than love. He pulled the pages from Zaniel out to find the final page was no longer blank. "I think Zaniel has provided the answer."

"Again."

They all looked around, but Zaniel didn't appear even as his voice continued.

"I can only help after you decide. Free will and all that."

Cabel was already scanning the page and Farren leaned in close to do the same. When Alida tried to edge in, the witches pulled her back.

There were multiple steps and they had covered a lot of them already. However, there were also vows and an exchange of gifts much like a human wedding.

"Do our blades count as our magical gifts? They respond to both of us."

"What blades?" Alida questioned as soon as Farren had finished speaking.

"Do you really want to talk about them crossing swords, Alida?"

His cousin groaned while the brothers laughed. Even Farren snorted at the exchange before he tapped one part of the page.

"I don't understand what this means."

He'd just been studying the same words, but Cabel smiled. "I think I do. Do you trust me?"

"I've already bound my fate to yours in a fairy duel so don't ask stupid questions, Princeling."

IT WAS STILL DARK WHEN Reid opened the door to his tattoo parlor. The human was scruffy and sleepy-eyed. "Not sure why this part of the bonding couldn't be done at a decent hour. Maybe after the sun had risen. I'm not a morning person."

Farren blushed at the words, but Cabel pushed him forward with a hand at his back. The final private step for their bonds had to take place at sunrise. It was their time.

"How will this work?" Farren spoke despite the heat coloring his face.

"The ink contains magic from your man's wings, and we used your potions. I'll ink the symbols you've chosen, but the final pictures come from magic and love." Reid tapped a pencil against the counter and appeared to be waking up as he gathered supplies. "I haven't done something quite like this, but I've seen magic change soulmate marks. I think this is the fairy version of that. Right, Cabel?"

He nodded once and followed the witch toward the back. "Essentially, yes. The ceremony calls for a symbolic magical exchange. Our blades were practical magical union."

"Still no need for those details even if Alida isn't here yet," Reid grumbled.

"You're good."

Farren didn't direct the comment at Cabel but instead at Reid. His human was studying the artwork decorating the walls of the room. It was easy to agree with his judgment. One particular image caught Cabel's eye and he stepped closer.

"What are you looking at?" Farren moved to press against Cabel's back to ask the question.

Reid glanced at them and then the image before turning away. "Some book or something inspired that. I can't even remember."

"Does it mean something to you? Is it magical?" Farren continued to look at the drawing as he took Cabel's hand in his.

Cabel watched the artist tense but the witch refused to turn around for the answer. "The symbols remind me of Dragons."

"Are we doing this or not?" Reid slammed the metal tray onto the table. "Who's first?"

Farren pulled the final ingredient from his bag and handed it to Cabel. "Guess I'll go first."

Chapter 22

It took little time to gain their magical marks from Reid. The sky was still dark when Cabel transported them back to Karsia. It was an easy trick since he had full control of his magic and understood the still-wild lands. They would have a few days to themselves before returning to Tellum for their Christmas ceremony with their family. A family that included his cousin, two witch brothers, and a Phoenix baby. He couldn't have imagined such a life, but it was the only one Cabel wanted, and he was anxious to start it.

"Shall we?" He offered a hand and Farren took it quickly. "We need to protect the land again and then bless the circle for our binding."

They did have to clear some of the space as the forest had encroached quickly. Working together with both blades out, they completed the task quickly. A small fire lit their circle while holly bushes provided relief from Karsia's heat. It wasn't as bad as before, but there was still work to be done. "We should ask Leina or Zaniel about building a portal between Tellum and Karsia. It'll make things easier."

"You see our future here?"

Cabel almost flinched at the question. "Your home is here. I know we didn't really talk about it."

"We haven't talked about much and I think we should."

FARREN KNEW HE'D SURPRISED his soon-to-be husband, but he had little time before the sun would rise. He had to be sure. "I need to tell you what Leina told me...and I have a gift for you."

The stiffness eased from Cabel's frame, and he nodded. Farren tried not to be distracted by the beauty of the fairy uniform or the fairy himself. He'd already gained enhanced vision though and it seemed wrong to waste it by not appreciating Cabel. He shook his head when he saw his lover staring at him expectantly. "Right, okay then."

He moved to sit on a surprisingly cushy boulder before realizing Cabel had reverted to the man he'd known and loved previously. "It was hard traveling with you the second time. I'd gotten used to us and there was no longer an us."

"I am sorry—"

"I know that, and I am too. That's why I need to tell you this." He reached for the strap crossing his chest and tugged on it. The magical buzz from his weapons had only grown stronger since the battle, and their cool presence calmed him. "It wasn't only because of Leina that I kept the truth from you."

Cabel didn't even blink at his words, so Farren rushed on.

"I'd seen *Agoen* and the wealth and beauty that surrounded you. I realized the chances of you slumming with me twice wasn't likely."

"Do not speak of yourself that way." Cabel's royal nature was released in all its glory as he stood to issue the order. "My life in *Agoen* was cold, lifeless. You're what I want. You're my choice."

He'd heard similar words from his lover, but not since Cabel had regained his memories. It brought a rush of pleasure and joy that allowed Farren to breathe easier. "That's good, because I couldn't walk away. I regretted telling Zaniel no before he'd even sent me crashing into the river. It was a relief when he brought me back. I'm glad I said no though."

His lover immediately understood and smiled. "You rescued Zoe that week. We wouldn't have her if you hadn't said no."

"You're good with having a family immediately. That wasn't something we'd discussed previously." Farren hadn't understood his bond to the child any more than his initial connection to a haughty prince.

Magic might have nudged him, but he'd also made a commitment to both. He wasn't able to walk away again and didn't want to try either. "I want us to be a family and that includes your crazy cousin and her witches and whoever else comes into our lives."

"Must we include the witches?"

Farren laughed at the suffering tone before he focused on Cabel dropping to a knee before him. "I won't tell them that you like them, but I think they know you aren't a spoiled royal ass."

"I don't want to talk about our family right now." Cabel's smile was still warm and wide. "I do want to talk about us. Is Zoe the only thing you're worried about?"

"You mean other than the sleeping supernatural lovers and the ongoing corruption in our lands? There are also human Hunters, Wolves who fight them, and something so bad happening in Epizo that people are risking their lives in Karsia to escape it." It was a longer list than he'd realized until speaking the words aloud. Farren huffed a laugh. "I've been all about surviving the last few years, but you make me want to live and enjoy life. I don't care about the list of issues, I care about us."

It was easy to accept the gentle kiss and revel in the unspoken promises it carried.

"I appreciate your practical nature, but I want you to have dreams and hopes. I want you to have everything." Cabel rested his forehead against Farren's and breathed the words against his lips. With just another brush of their mouths together, his lover pulled back.

"Funny you should mention that. I have a gift for you." Farren pulled his back closer and dug inside. The hastily wrapped gift was heavy in his hands. "Alida helped me create it 'cause it's not like I could find someone who had it for barter."

As if the brown, crinkled paper was precious, Cabel unwrapped it slowly. Farren waited as patiently as he could for those silver-blue eyes to meet his.

"It's beautiful."

"I realized you were willing to stay here before and more so now, and I wanted you to have something good from your homeland. I know Rister was a bag of troll nuts, but you have good memories of *Agoen* and I'd like us to visit it. I'd like us to take Zoe there when she's older." Farren forced himself to stop rambling.

The snow globe was a recreation of the snowy lake they'd spent several days at when Cabel had taken him to *Agoen*. The crackling pink-orange fire and red and green holly bushes were the only colors in the glowing scene. It had been important to include them all.

"It's beautiful and I'll treasure it always. I'd be honored to take you and Zoe to *Agoen* in the future. Our home is here now, but I like knowing where I started so I could get here. I hope you'll like my gift as much as I love yours."

The relief coursing through Farren meant he almost missed the last words. "Gift? You got a gift for me?"

"Yes, and it appears we had a similar thought." Cabel moved the globe to open hand just before another one appeared. He offered it to Farren without explanation.

Dropping his gaze to the gift, Farren gasped. Karsia was well-represented with lush greenery, a blue river, and even golden sand. It was the recreation of his weapon and their *reweial* crossed in the orange sky that made the scene magical.

"I thought I understood what it meant to be a warrior, to live and die with honor. I was wrong." Cabel cupped Farren's hands in his and gently shook the snow globe. Pink sparkles lit the scene instead of concealing it. "You're the real magic in my life."

Later, he would be embarrassed by their sappy exchange. Now, Farren placed the globe on the ground and tackled his lover. The familiar hard body under his was a fantastic distraction from the strum of emotions roiling inside him. Their kisses and touches grew more frantic until the rising sun nearly blinded them.

"Okay, okay. Magical gift-giving time now." Farren nipped at Cabel's earlobe before pulling back completely. "I do want to see how these tattoos play out. What if I get a dick pic on my forehead? I won't be happy with you."

"That's how you think our bond will be expressed? A dick pic?" Cabel kissed his forehead and then pulled Farren up with him as he stood.

Shrugging, Farren tried to imitate the poker face his lover frequently used. "The sex is great. magical even so it's a possibility."

"Only one way to find out," Cabel agreed with his princely visage in place...until he winked.

It seemed fitting they entered the smaller circle holding hands as Farren rolled his eyes. Flames immediately encircled them before the fire became interlocking snowflakes. The small altar in the center contained their offerings of holly berries, pine combs, and river rocks. Kneeling next to it, they intertwined their free hands and smiled.

"Earth grounds fire and air softens water. Peace needs love as love needs hope. We offer all that we are and all that we will become to be bound together until we are no more. As we will so mote it be."

It was exhilarating and humbling to repeat the vow while staring at his fairy. Joy filled Farren...until the pain knocked the breath out of him.

His back felt like it was on fire and Farren jerked upright before crashing back down. Cabel released a growling whimper. Farren wanted to reach for him, but the pain kept him locked in place. Black dots filled the periphery of his vision and then inched closer; he welcomed the reprieve.

It was his lover's touch to his face that finally woke Farren.

"There you are. Breathe for me, love. It's okay." Cabel stroked his face and smiled down at him. "Are you still in pain?"

Surprisingly, there wasn't even an echo of the fiery torture. He sat up and shook his head. "No, actually. It would have been nice if someone had mentioned that part though. Did you..." Green and gold bands now glistened on his lover's wrists. Farren touched the intricately designed cuffs and glanced up to find Cabel smiling proudly.

"My ink is beautiful but yours is beyond stunning." The smile became mischievous before Cabel chuckled. "Stand up and see."

Farren followed the advice and glanced down at his body as he stood. There was no magically inked jewelry on his wrists...but he was shirtless. "What the fox? I don't see anything. What do I have?"

"I think you need to check your back." Cabel's face was a blank mask.

When he twisted to look over his shoulder, a large golden wing flapped and hit him in the face. Farren turned completely around but no one, nothing had violated their circle to attack. His love's laughter had him turning back again only to have another collision with feathers. Before he could spin around, Cabel grasped his hips to still him. Farren wanted to glare, but his fairy's face glowed with delight.

"Will you let me help you?"

"Yes, yes," Farren agreed with a wave of his hand. A mirror appeared in that hand. The reflection showed another mirror behind him...and an enormous pair of golden wings. "Are you telling me I have wings now?"

"Yours appear like a Pegasus, but yes, we both have wings."

Farren continued to look from the mirror to his lover. "Wait, I thought it was supposed to be a tattoo. I can't walk around with these out. You can hide yours."

Stepping even closer, Cabel stroked a hand down Farren's spine, and the wings disappeared. It was then he could see the inked version of the appendages. The mere thought of the other version had them popping out again. This time, there was only a little pain. That pain became pleasure when he felt Cabel touch several of the feathers. The pleasure only intensified when fairy wings brushed against his own.

"Your wings are out." Farren paused to appreciate that revelation. All three sets glistened with an ethereal beauty that put the real-world sunrise to shame.

"No, they aren't. I suspect the bond allows you to see them as I can feel your heartbeat." Cabel's attention was directed just over Farren's shoulders. "I wonder if you'll appreciate my touch on your wings as much as I appreciate yours."

YES, FARREN DID ENJOY both aspects of his wing kink. Round two happened with the sun soaring in the sky and their bodies suspended mid-air.

"Why don't I take the lead as your wings are new?"

His lover's arms were around his waist and Cabel smiled sweetly at him. Farren nodded without speaking as his wings flapped behind him.

"We aren't far from the ground, and I won't let you fall."

Even the warm sun and the cooler breeze against his sensitive wings sent a shiver down Farren's spine. He couldn't resist moving one hand to tug gently on one of Cabel's mating wings. His lover had much more control over his wings but touching his mating pair did make the man moan.

"If you keep distracting me, we'll never join the mile-high club," Cabel teased.

"Not a mile. We're staying here, just hovering. Between the wings and the orgasm, I may pass out." He offered it as a joke, but Farren was almost sure he would.

Cabel brushed his lips over Farren's and smiled. "I'll always take care of you, *Imisi*."

"Let's do it."

His lover took the words seriously and ran a hand through Farren's wings even as the other one stroked up to tweak a nipple. By the time that hand moved down to caress his cock, Farren had to grip Cabel's shoulders tightly. His wings flared before beating a fast rhythm that lifted them higher. Before he could look down, Cabel cupped his face and kissed him again. When he needed air, his love simply continued his loving assault on other places on his body.

"So beautiful." Soft kisses covered his face and Farren kept his eyes closed.

"Such a good heart. I can feel our love in every beat." Hands moved to rest over his heart before Cabel's tongue flicked against his nipple. Laughter was breathed into his skin. "I can also feel how it leaps when I touch you."

There was nowhere to hide but Farren kept his eyes closed even as his heart did thud against his ribs.

"I want to bring you as much pleasure as you bring me, more if such is even possible." Teeth tugging his nipple almost made Farren miss the sneaky finger rubbing at his hole. A rush of cooling air left him wet and relaxed as his lover's magic always brought bliss.

Still floating with his eyes closed, Farren had no warning when Cabel's mouth swallowed him without preamble. Hot, sucking pressure had his eyes rolling back and his back arching. Only then did his fairy pull back. Soft licks now teased the sensitive tip of his cock. His hands found soft hair and Farren tugged gently.

"So sweet and good...and all for me."

A finger pressed deep inside as the heat of his lover's mouth surrounded him again. Even his wings pulsed and tingled with pleasure. Before he could orgasm too quickly, Cabel pulled back once more.

"I crave your heat and fire with a need I didn't know was possible."

Farren had enjoyed sex before Cabel, but his fairy made it magical in every way. He couldn't help but beg for more. "Please, please."

More soft kisses on his stomach and thighs. A twist and curl of the fingers buried deep inside him brought a strangled cry.

"Yes, my love. I think you're ready too. I know I can't wait any longer to complete our union."

Gravity meant little as Cabel bent Farren's legs and moved up his body for another kiss. Now, he could clutch his love close even as they flew higher.

"You are stunning in every way, and I love you." Cabel thrust into Farren's body with ease.

Wrapping his legs around his lover's hips, Farren met his movements with a new angle. His body hummed with pleasure, hot and magical. "I love you too."

"Will you look at me, *Imisi*?"

Only a request from Cabel could have pulled Farren's eyes open. Silver rimmed black when he met his fairy's gaze. The words tumbled out again. "I love you."

He couldn't hear anything but the roar of blood in his ears as his orgasm washed over him. Farren's eyes closed again when he felt Cabel follow him over the edge. Together, they floated, blissful and satisfied.

Epilogue

Cabel frowned at the snow covering Tellum when they arrived at the Debare family home. It had snowed every year since their bonding ceremony...and since Alida had bet that it would. They had continued to celebrate their anniversary privately before joining for the holiday celebration in Tellum. Every year, it was the same thing. "You should have brought a jacket."

Rolling his eyes, Farren stepped through the gate first. "It's still warm in Karsia so I don't need a jacket. It looks like Leina added more flowers this year."

The witch had helped them create a *lanua* to link Tellum and Karsia. There were several gates including a private one they used for such events. Zoe raced forward with a gleeful cry and Alida followed closely behind. Farren moved more quickly to greet their daughter. Cabel flicked his wrist to cover his husband with a warm coat before embracing his cousin.

"I'm so glad you're here. You've gotta teach Zoe not to set things on fire before she starts human school. She was not happy with her cousins destroying her dollhouse."

His cousin had never learned to whisper so his daughter turned to glare at her while Farren chuckled.

"He almost broke my snow globe," Zoe defended herself. She threw herself into Cabel's arms. "I did warn him, Papa."

That was her name for him, and warmth flooded his heart as he hugged the little girl. There was no way he'd punish her for protecting herself.

"Those globes are pretty tough, but I'm not sure they'd survive if you burned the house down. Not to mention your aunts and uncles would be very sad, Spark."

Farren chastised gently before Cabel could let her off the hook. He couldn't deny his husband any more than he could his daughter, so Cabel stayed quiet. Zoe dropped her head against his shoulder and pressed into his neck. He turned pleading eyes to Farren.

"I think you owe him an apology." Farren paused and held Cabel's gaze as Zoe sniffled loudly. "And then we'll open Phyllia's present which you know means chocolate."

Zoe squirmed to the ground and danced around them. Small orange sparkles followed her every step. She grabbed Farren's hand and then Cabel's and pulled them both forward. "Come on, Auntie A, I'll share my chocolate with you."

Alida's laughter followed them toward the house. "I do not like burnt chocolate, Zoe! Be nice to your favorite Aunt please."

Adults and children rushed out to greet them with open arms and welcoming magic as they arrived at the front door.

Farren didn't have to wait a single heartbeat before his husband and daughter spoke in unison, "And a very fairy Christmas to all!"

Author's Note

If you need more gay romantic tropes set in a magical world, I hope you'll check out my other books available now. Please also consider leaving a review and giving me a follow to learn of new releases.

Thanks and have a very fairy Christmas this year!

-Tiana

TROPES ARE US READING Order:

Purrfect Healing

Single Wolf Omega

Knock on Wood

A new Dragon story is coming soon!

Made in the USA
Las Vegas, NV
17 December 2024

14445658R00079